"I'll soon have this marriage annulled!"

"Ma...marriage?" Victor's eyes turned from her father to Venetia as suspicion dawned.

"Please, Father. You must let me explain—" But Venetia's words were lost in the torrent of epithets her father rained down upon her head.

"There is nothing to explain. I'll have the law on you, Allen! Never again will any respectable lady of Quality be lured to sit for you in this den of iniquity!"

"No, Papa! It is not true that Mr. Allen married—" But again Venetia's words were silenced as she found herself pulled roughly into Allen's embrace.

"Hush, my sweet," he murmured, his mouth closing over hers. "Your father does not believe that it is love which has bound us together. But no one, and certainly not you, sir, can tear us asunder!"

Regency England: 1811-1820

"It was the best of times, it was the worst of times...."
As George III languished in madness, the pampered
and profligate Prince of Wales led the land in revelry
and the elegant Beau Brummel set the style. Across
the Channel, Napoleon continued to plot against the
English until his final exile to St. Helena. Across the
Atlantic, America renewed hostilities with an old
adversary, declaring war on Britain in 1812. At
home, Society glittered, love matches abounded and
poets such as Lord Byron flourished. It was a time of
heroes and villains, a time of unrelenting charm and
gaiety, when entire fortunes were won or lost on a
turn of the dice and reputation was all. A dazzling
period that left its mark on two continents and
whose very name became a byword for elegance
and romance.

Books by Eva Rutland

HARLEQUIN REGENCY ROMANCE

GRETNA BRIDE

EVA RUTLAND

Harlequin Books

TORONTO • NEW YORK • LONDON
AMSTERDAM • PARIS • SYDNEY • HAMBURG
STOCKHOLM • ATHENS • TOKYO • MILAN
MADRID • WARSAW • BUDAPEST • AUCKLAND

To my husband and my love, for all the fun

Published January 1993

ISBN 0-373-31189-3

GRETNA BRIDE

Printed in U.S.A.

CHAPTER ONE

THE ELEGANT, immaculately polished barouche rolled easily over the cobbles and stopped at 41 Fitzroy Square. The footman jumped down from his perch to open the carriage door and let down the steps to allow a maidservant to alight. Then both lifted their hands to assist their young mistress.

Venetia Fielding paused in progress with one of her small satin slippered feet resting on the bottom step, to disdainfully survey her location. The tall Town houses surrounding the square were all in a row, the porches leading directly onto the street. No gardens, trees or shrubs and only a few raggedy blossoms bravely straggled from the two or three window-boxes in evidence. Across the square three filthy urchins engaged in a game of sticks and hoops. A fishmonger glanced at the elegant barouche as he wheeled his cart around it. Doors in the square opened as several women emerged, summoned by his hawking...

"Haddock, fresh haddock."

Venetia descended from the carriage and was accompanied to her destination. Glancing up, she noted that the sign she sought was partially covered by weeds. Yet she could still decipher the words, Victor Allen, Portraits. The precise flowing script could have been impressive had the brass plate not been dulled by dust and hung at such a rakish angle. She sighed as she gestured for Hudson to apply his hand to the door knocker. Why, she had asked Papa, had he insisted that her portrait be painted by this particular artist?

"I've seen the one he did of Sutcliffe's daughter, Eliza" was his reply. "Plainer they don't come but Allen painted her pretty. Stands to reason he'd make a raving beauty out of you!"

But any painter would do that, Venetia thought. Not because she was vain. Her red-gold hair, brilliant green eyes, fair skin and perfect features had been remarked upon so often that she had long since learned to accept her beauty as a pleasant fact. Inconceivable that any artist would diminish undeniable beauty. Still her father had insisted on Victor Allen.

"It must be done to perfection, you know. Our wedding gift to His Grace so you may take your place among all those other fancy ladies lining his gallery at Lynderly." His face took on the gloating look of one who had just won a coveted prize. "Imagine...my daughter as Her Grace, Duchess of Hazlemere. Oh, I can't wait to see their tonnish faces when we announce your betrothal."

Venetia smiled dreamily. But only one face sprang to her mind. *His.* Her heart sang... *Bertram, I love you. Always you.* She would love him even if he were poor and they had to live in a cottage or even, heaven forbid, in such a hovel as this.

"Seems nobody's to home," Maggie, the maid, remarked, as they stood on the porch listening to the silence within. Hudson again applied the knocker, louder this time.

"Give it a good whack!" called a voice from the street. They looked to see a common woman waving her fish at them. "I know he's to home. Don't pay no mind to nothin' once he's up there dippin' in them paint pots. And Bella's deaf as a post. Give it a good hard thwack!"

Hudson lifted his hand to do just that when the door was flung open by a girl of about fifteen. She wiped her hands on a rather soiled apron and did not take Venetia's card. But in answer to Hudson's announcing that Miss Fielding had an appointment with Mr. Allen, she gestured towards a wide staircase.

"Just go up. Top floor." Seeming surprised by their hesitation, she assured them, "He's there, all right. He'll be waitin' for ya."

This was too much. Not even a mere footman properly assigned to attend the door and to escort his guest to his master's studio. But when Papa was set on something... Venetia shrugged and instructed Hudson to see to the horses and return in two hours. Then, accompanied by Maggie, she entered the dismal hall.

"That way, miss. Then go 'cross the hall and up one more flight to the next landing. He be there." The girl seemed inclined to escort them, but in response to a bellow from somewhere below demanding her to "get down here and see to these potatoes!" she scurried away.

The house, seemingly so silent as they had waited outside, now became a noisy hub. As Maggie and Venetia proceeded up the stairs, the shouting from below still reverberated as some woman advised the unfortunate Annie to be quick about this or that. A nattily attired young man jauntily descending the stairs doffed his hat, eyeing them appreciatively as he passed. Once Venetia and her maid had reached the first landing, more sounds could be heard behind closed doors—voices of two women raised in argument, a man's gruff pleading tones, a girl's giggle. Venetia gave Maggie a speaking look. Clearly this was no place for a lady and she meant to tell her Papa so.

"Mr. Fielding did request that Mr. Allen come to your house," Maggie whispered as if in response to Venetia's silent disgust. "Right put out your pa was when I overheard him telling the missus that the arrogant jackanapes had flatly refused! Begging your pardon, Miss Venetia, but your pa's very words were 'the bloody bastard won't be budged.'"

True. Venetia had herself read the politely phrased artist's message of regret…"Impossible to work in any but the best conditions."

Well! If this old character considered this the "best"—

A merry whistle carrying the melody of a popular song interrupted her musings as a young man bounded down the steps, almost bumping into her.

"*Pardon, mademoiselle,*" he apologized. He shifted a number of portfolios he was carrying beneath one arm and bowed, moving aside as he did so and gesturing aloft. "Please, Monsieur Allen awaits." He appeared unabashed by Venetia's icy nod, and they heard him resume his merry whistle as he continued his inelegant descent.

The third staircase was narrow and steep. Venetia gripped the bannister as she ascended. At the top landing, open double doors led into a large room, smelling strongly of paints. To her amazement the wall which should have been to her left, as well as a portion of the roof, was composed entirely of windows, and as the sun pouring through was so bright, she was forced to shade her eyes.

"In a moment, *s'il vous plait.*" The disembodied voice she heard was husky, pleasant, with a definite French accent. Squinting, Venetia was able to see a man disposing of a canvas against the far wall. Then he turned and Venetia gasped. This tall figure of a man in black trousers that accentuated his lean hips, wearing a white shirt, open at the collar with his sleeves rolled up to display strong forearms, was no old character!

"Bonjour, mesdemoiselles." His greeting was designed to welcome them both, before he turned his attention on Venetia. "And you are Mademoiselle...?" He paused as if trying to recall whom he was commissioned to paint that morning.

"Fielding. Venetia Fielding," she supplied, as she considered his clean-shaven jawline and sensitive dark eyes. Young, she thought, probably still in his twenties. He could be handsome, she had to admit, but a smudge of paint bruising one high cheekbone and his tangle of black hair made him appear unattractively unkempt.

"Ah, yes, Miss Fielding. Well, then. Take off your cloak and let me have a look at you," he said pleasantly.

Venetia tossed back her hood and unclasped the garment, handing it to Maggie. Turning around to face him, she fully expected and was poised to receive with grace the compliments always bestowed upon her.

She was taken aback by his frown. He was not looking at her with admiration at all, but with a detached sort of consideration.

"It will not do," he said, shaking his head. "Not at all."

"Oh?" Venetia muttered, somewhat abashed.

"The dress, all those furbelows. Too much clutter."

Clutter! Her gaze swept over the room with its hotchpotch of bottles, jars, brushes and Lord knew what else lying about. She stared pointedly at a vase of dried-up flowers, a pair of discarded gloves, a fan, dirty rags and all kinds of debris piled on a large trestle table. *Clutter, indeed!* As if he knew the meaning of the word! Her gown had cost Papa a fortune.

"You do not understand," she said tartly. "This dress was especially designed for me to wear for my sitting as it shall be hung in the gallery at—" She broke off, remembering just in time that her engagement was not yet official. "It is to be hung in a very important place."

"Not with *my* signature." With that he dismissed the matter as he instructed her maidservant where to hang their coats and where to sit while she waited for her mistress. "Now, Miss Fielding, if you would step forward a little, towards the light."

Automatically Venetia moved as he bade, but turned towards him, her face burning with indignation. Madame Fanchot was the best modiste in London and certainly knew a great deal more about style than did this hapless artist who could easily be mistaken for a common street vendor.

"Mr. Allen," she said crisply, running a hand over the smooth gold satin of her skirt. "This dress is in the first stare of fashion."

"Undoubtedly," he agreed absently. Then, from the cluttered table, he took up a sketch-book and stared fixedly at her. "Tilt your chin a trifle, please."

Venetia tilted her chin, but her eyes shot daggers at him. Odious man!

"I am compelled to inform you, sir, that unless Papa is perfectly satisfied, you should not expect to receive any compensation for your efforts."

"Naturally." He fumbled under the debris on the table to unearth a charcoal crayon and, seating himself on a stool, he began to sketch rapidly.

Venetia grew more livid. This arrogant man needed a set-down! If he knew for whom this portrait was intended, he would— Her musings were interrupted by a noise on the stairs consisting of bumps, grunts and laboured breathing, as if a heavy object were being dragged up. Turning, she saw a dirty dishevelled urchin emerge into the room carrying a barrel almost as big as he.

"Here 'tis, sir. All right and tight."

"Good lad, Oliver. Set it against the wall there and take sixpence for yourself." Allen continued on with his sketching, not even glancing at the boy as he dug into a big bowl on the trestle table, pushing aside what appeared to be notes and drafts to select his own coin.

"Thank you, sir. If you like, I could get down to Terry's afore he—"

"Not today, my boy. Tell Bella to give you a bit of breakfast and be off with you."

With unintelligible words of gratitude, the boy scurried off. Allen rose from his stool and brought a chair forward for her.

"Sit here, *mademoiselle,* if you please. I'd like to sketch you from a different angle."

At last, she thought, sinking into the proffered chair which had been indicated not out of courtesy but for his own convenience. Not only was she forced to travel to his quarters, but it appeared as though he meant to insist she be constantly moving about or bobbing up and down like some jumping jack!

"Are you not happy, Miss Fielding?"

"Happy?" She frowned, resenting his temerity. If he but knew that she, Venetia Fielding, was soon to become betrothed to her darling Bertram, he could not have asked such a foolish question. "Of course I'm happy," she said with a touch of irritation.

Victor Allen smiled. "Would you elaborate for me," he said as he resumed his seat on the stool.

"About what?"

"Whatever makes you happy."

She hesitated. Papa had sworn her to secrecy; no announcement was to be made until the betrothal party when he said he meant to "give those toadeaters something to bow and scrape about." Keeping her pledge was particularly hard for Venetia, who felt like an air balloon about to lift off and discover the wonders of Heaven. She wanted everyone to know. Her only confidante had been Emma Linton, for how could she keep the wonderful earth-shattering secret from her bosom friend! Emma had herself just received an offer from Lord Stewart. Not nearly so eligible a *parti* as Venetia's duke, but a love match, as well. She and Emma had spent many happy hours poring over Mrs. Radcliffe's romantic novels and vowing to each other that neither would ever wed unless really and truly in love. And now the dream had come true for both of them . . . like a miracle!

"Parfait! Stay just as you are," coaxed the artist. "Whatever you are thinking brings such a warm bloom to your cheeks and a joyful sparkle to your eyes!" He was watching her and sketching rapidly as he spoke. "Excellent. Your happiness is apparent, *mademoiselle.*"

"Oh, yes," she agreed breathlessly. She had to tell someone. And this raggedy artist was not one of the ton. "It is a secret as yet, so you must not breathe a word of it to anyone," she cautioned. "I am to wed this fall." When he received this whispered confession with only a slightly raised eyebrow, she added, impressively in her full voice, "To His Grace, The Duke of Hazlemere."

"I see." This time he inclined his head in a slight acknowledgement as he flipped over a leaf and employed his charcoal crayon to make several more quick strokes. "A most estimable match."

"Yes, but . . ." Venetia faltered, irked by his negligent tone but hesitant to blurt out that theirs was a real love match. And, of course, it *was* an estimable match. Mama was beside herself with joy. "Oh, my

precious child," she had crowed. "To think you have
made the greatest catch. All those dowagers with eligible daughters have been setting their caps at the duke
for ages. Simply ages and to no avail. He has offered
for you, my angel . . . in your first Season and barely
past your seventeenth year."

As if he had been waiting just for her, Venetia
thought. For it had been love at first sight for both of
them—just like in Mrs. Radcliffe's novels. There had
been no thought given to his title or her lack of one.
The ballroom had been crowded, yet they had found
each other in an instant. Even now she could remember how he had bent his handsome face towards hers,
how his luminous grey eyes had beckoned so mysteri-
ously and how her whole being had responded to that
unspoken message.

"*Bon!* The smile . . . *c'est agréable!* Your Hazlemere . . . quite a formidable gentleman."

"More than a gentleman! I told you. He is a duke!"

"So you did. And so fortunate a one to have engaged such devotion. Handsome, I presume, and
dashing?" Allen's voice was like a magnet attaching
itself to her soul and urging her to divulge her heart's
innermost secrets. As in a dream she began to pour out
her expressions of love for Bertram.

The sound of running footsteps abruptly returned
her to reality. This time the servant girl, Annie, entered the room, looking rather harassed.

"Mr. Allen, you said that if Josie should leave that
I could have her room. Well, sir, Bert's sent her
packin' again, but she came back and said I gotta go
'cause she were there first." The wretched girl paused

for breath, snivelling and wiping her nose on her sleeve. A fat tear rolled down her cheek as she wailed.

"Oh, do stop that snivelling, Annie. We shall manage something. Now be gone with you."

"But Cook says..." The girl hesitated, reluctant to leave without complete assurances.

"Never you mind Bella. I'll see to her." Satisfied now, the girl proceeded to leave, having to dodge past a burly man with a scar on one cheek and a scarf round his neck. He doffed his hat and made an elaborate bow to Venetia before addressing Allen.

"Pardon, guv'nor. Don't like to take ya from your work, but I'd best give you your stake back afore it slips through me fingers."

"High water with you, then is it?" The artist smiled but did not look up from his sketch-book.

"Swimmin' in it! Ivories stuck with me the whole blessed night. Lucky stake you give me. So I brung it right back." So saying, the burly man took a roll of notes from his pocket.

"Thank you, my good man. Drop it over there in the bowl, if you will."

Venetia watched in amazement as the man lumbered across to the trestle table and dropped the notes into the same bowl whence the urchin had removed his sixpence. Good gracious! This "artist" must be queer in the attic to keep an open cash-box, convenient for any or all to deposit or dip into at will! Most improvident, she thought, as the abominable creature reappeared at her side to execute another bow before he made his departure.

Incredible that Mr. Allen could continue to paint while a menagerie of humanity appeared at will, demanding or disturbing as they chose. No, not disturbing, she thought. For nothing seemed to disturb Mr. Allen's equanimity or his concentration.

But his methods were most peculiar. Not at all like those of Sir Thomas Lawrence, who had painted her mama's portrait. Sir Thomas had presented himself at their front door dressed in the impeccable attire of a gentleman, but once shown into the sitting-room he had donned his smock-frock and had immediately set up his easel and paint pots. Having done so, Sir Thomas had seen her mama comfortably settled upon her own sofa wearing the gown that she had carefully selected, before he had begun to paint.

Victor Allen had yet to touch a paint pot. He continued to sketch with charcoal, though he must have compiled a dozen or more likenesses of her already. At this rate she would be forced to return and return . . .

"Do not lower your head, please." Mr. Allen had leapt from his stool and now stood before her. She stared at him, her eyes narrowing in disdain.

"Your eyes wider, please. Yes, lovely, *mademoiselle*. Now you must raise your brows. There." So compelling was his voice, so magnetic were his dark unfathomable eyes and the penetrating gaze that he had fixed upon her that she could only return his regard. It was he who finally looked away. Still somewhat stunned, Venetia watched in silence as he crossed to the trestle table and at last selected some paint pots. But surely he did not intend to begin her portrait, for there was no canvas in evidence. Instead, he balanced a small wooden palette in the crook of his elbow as he mixed the paints.

"Mr. Allen," she said, "I do hope you understand that this portrait is to be completed with all speed."

Mr. Allen nodded.

"It is to be ready to be hung in His Grace's gallery at Lynderly as soon as..." Her voice trailed away as he again approached her and looked down into her face.

"Mr. Allen, if you would just listen."

"You will look at me, *s'il vous plaît*. Open your eyes wider. Ah." He returned to the table, dabbing furiously with his brush. "Wonderful!" he finally announced and once again settled on his stool and was instantly absorbed in his work.

This was the outside of enough. The wretched man didn't heard a word she said or was, worse still, deliberately snubbing her! Venetia gestured towards Maggie, who had been watching the proceedings with interest from her nearby chair. "Fetch our cloaks, Maggie. We are leaving." When she returned home she would tell her papa that he must fetch Sir Thomas Lawrence, for she had no intention of returning to this ramshackle house which could not under any circumstances be considered the residence of a professional artist.

"A moment, *mademoiselle*." Victor Allen had walked across the room and now handed her a leaf from his sketch-book. "If you would instruct your modiste to design such a dress in exactly such a colour."

Venetia stared at the illustration, somewhat awed by the rapidity with which he had sketched it and fascinated by the beautiful shade of green . . . or was it turquoise?

"She must be persuaded to finish it immediately. That is the dress which you will wear for your sitting...and she must make it up in a soft material, silk or velvet, nothing else."

Venetia stiffened. His manner was inexcusable. "What you will wear" indeed! He had not bothered with "I should like," or "if it should please you." Such impertinence!

"Mr. Allen," she said firmly. "This will not do. You fail to understand that we have already selected this gown at some expense and with much consideration for my sitting." She touched her hand to the sequined collarette. "It is perhaps difficult for you to apprehend what is fashionable, sir, for you are not a famous modiste!"

"No. I am a painter, *mademoiselle*. I paint the lady, not the decorations."

"But surely even a mere painter could discern that this gown you prefer is too plain," she said indignantly. "It . . . it is like a bed cloth!"

"Indeed. And it will fall softly to mold the loveliness of your figure."

Venetia gasped at such effrontery. But once again she felt herself the object of detached appraisal rather than admiration. Still, wasn't it disrespectful to make such a bold reference to her figure? And shouldn't she . . . ?

"See here," he said, pointing to the corsage of his selected gown. "Such a line will allow the full display of the graceful contours of your neck and chin and greatly enhance your lovely profile. You are an exceptionally beautiful woman, *mademoiselle.*"

"Oh," said Venetia in a small voice. She who had heard these same words of praise many, many times. Why then did it seem as if she now heard them for the first time?

"And the colour, *mademoiselle,* it cannot be too exact. It must reflect the colour of your eyes and not do battle with your glorious blaze of hair."

"Oh," she said again.

"So. You will tell your modiste to do exactly as in the painting? *Oui?*"

"Oui," agreed Mademoiselle Fielding, noticing of a sudden that Mr. Allen had a very sweet smile.

CHAPTER TWO

"I AM SURPRISED that your father permits your visits to Fitzroy Square," Miss Linton said as she led Venetia into her bedchamber sitting-room.

"Ha! Were he aware of the goings-on there, I am persuaded he would not. But Mama has become immersed in preparations for my betrothal ball, so I am accompanied only by my abigail, Maggie, who will not reveal a thing we see or hear." Venetia allowed a gurgle of laughter to escape her as she settled herself on the chaise longue. "Really, Emma, I find Mr. Allen's household vastly entertaining. Somewhat like watching a farce at Covent Garden."

Emma paused in the act of displaying for her friend's inspection the bolts of muslin and silk which had been selected for her bride clothes. "Oh, Venetia, you cannot have heard of Mr. Longbourne, then. He is the darling of the ton just now, and everyone simply must have him to paint their portrait or perish. But the tabbies have it that he must indulge in all sorts of nodcock antics in order to paint. They say he went into raptures over Lucinda Connelly's beauty, which we all know to be only passable, yet the finished portrait made the poor girl look a positive dowd!

You cannot mean to say that your Mr. Allen is anything like—"

"Oh, heavens no, you goose! I assure you that Mr. Allen performs no antics and would never go into raptures. He simply stares and frowns and sketches, all the while issuing orders to sit this way or that."

"But you said it was like watching a—"

"No, silly, I did not mean Mr. Allen. I meant all those freakish creatures that are forever coming and going."

"Creatures?"

"Pray do not be such a slowtop. People, Emma. But not the kind of persons you or I would ever be likely to meet. On the very first day, I encountered the most burly man with a huge scar who affected the most courtly manners. But I was not to be taken in, for his dress and speech clearly marked him a bounder from the streets. Indeed I would have thought him a highwayman or a footpad except it seems he makes a living from ivories."

"Ivories?" Emma set the bolts of muslin and silk on top of her dressing table and sat down to give her full attention to her friend.

"I don't know precisely what ivories are," Venetia puzzled. "Or how he uses them. But as I understand it, if they stay with him all night he always brings back his stake."

"Stake?"

"The money he borrows from Mr. Allen, presumably to use the ivories I know not how."

"I see," said Emma rather dubiously. "It does indeed sound a peculiar business. But it is bound to be above suspicion as there was no indication of concealment.''

"None," agreed Venetia eagerly. "In point of fact, Victor Allen and this creature were conversing on the same subject just days ago when Lord Axley happened in at the same time. You are acquainted with Lord Axley, are you not? He is a dear friend of my mama's and has been married this age to Lady Frances, but I fear he is a pompous popinjay. But the good Lord Axley was most anxious to conceal his *own* business!" Venetia leaned forward and spoke confidentially. "He told Mr. Allen he had come to pick up the portrait that he had commissioned, but when he saw me he immediately and quite pointedly advised Mr. Allen that he would leave his bank draught and collect the painting next day. I vow it was very likely a portrait of that fancy piece he is said to keep at that love nest of his!"

"No doubt. Poor Lady Frances." Emma shook her head before asking with eager curiosity, "Did you get a peek? Surely the portrait must have been in the room at the time. His *chère amie* is rumoured to be a great beauty."

"Well, as to that I cannot say, for I did not see so much as a corner of it. Allen did as he always does. He simply nodded and kept on sketching. He barely attended to Lord Axley when he dropped his draught into the bowl on the table and then quickly took his leave."

"Dropped his draught into a bowl?" enquired Miss Linton, who had some difficulty absorbing the meaning.

Venetia giggled at both her friend's reaction and the nonsensical explanation to come. "Yes. Can you credit it? Mr. Allen employs the bowl as a sort of cash-box that sits as bold as brass on his big table. It's full to brimming with all kinds of currency; notes, draughts and coins. *And,* this is the part that shall surely surprise you as it did me. Mr. Allen invites everyone who comes and goes to either contribute as agreed to the cash-box or remove whatever they wish to borrow or have in some way earned." Venetia then described the various persons who had thus far availed themselves of Mr. Allen's generosity and watched as Emma's eyes widened in disbelief.

"I do believe your Mr. Allen is what my brother would call a loose screw."

"Indeed he is not!" Venetia declared rather hotly. Though she had perhaps thought so herself, she found she did not care for anyone else to say so. "He's just...well, different."

"But he cannot be a sensible man to keep his money in such a hare-brained fashion."

"You may think so, Emma, but I'm persuaded he does so as he cares so little about money. Papa offered him a much larger fee if he'd come to the house to paint my portrait. And he flatly refused."

"That, too, is incomprehensible. You must know that Sir Thomas, a very respected portrait artist, will always come to one's house, and when he came here to paint Mama's portrait, he would not allow a soul near the drawing-room. I do not understand how your Mr. Allen can do good work with all those interruptions."

"Emma, I have told you. Mr. Allen does not notice any interruptions. If you saw him at work you would put all doubts aside. He is forever frowning in concentration, except for when he smiles if he is pleased. He is very earnest, and says he must look into the soul to see what to paint. Many times he has fixed his dark eyes upon me with such a penetrating gaze. And then he speaks in such coaxing tones that you find yourself confiding your deepest thoughts and feelings to him. Besides yourself, he is the only one I've told about Bertram and me."

"Oh, Venetia, you didn't! Your papa will be incensed."

"I shouldn't worry. I know Mr. Allen will keep my confidence. In fact, he encourages me to speak of Bertram because when I do so, there comes a special sparkle to my eyes."

"But what of other people who frequent Mr. Allen's house? For instance, Lord Axley."

"Oh, Emma, really. Of course we do not speak of intimate things when other people are about."

"All the same, I cannot think that your Mr. Allen has behaved wisely. From the goings-on you have described, I would hardly expect that he would attract wealthy patrons of any consequence."

Venetia stopped to consider this but was forced to conclude that Mr. Allen cared nothing for consequence.

"Here's the thing," she said finally. "I think that just as Mr. Allen cares so little for money, he cares so much more for people."

"But did you not just say that he never heeds them?"

"Not precisely. He may not let them take him from his work, but he does hear everything that is said." And what is more, she thought, knows what each needs. He knew the urchin, Oliver, was hungry, and that Annie needed to be comforted. "He is a kind and caring man."

"Venetia Fielding, I do believe you have developed a *tendre* for him."

"Oh, Emma! How can you say so! When you of all people know my truest heart. As if I could ever give a single thought to anyone but my darling Bertram." Suffused with a guilty flush, she felt compelled to explain her regard for Victor Allen further. "If you must know, it is just that I am persuaded Mr. Allen is too kind and too trusting. People will make too much of a good thing. In point of fact, there is a certain one I can name. A flaxen-haired creature that comes almost every day. She is very beautiful with skin as pale and smooth as porcelain and with the most fetching blue eyes." Here Venetia paused, uncomfortably aware she had strayed from the topic. "Of course," she continued more firmly, "she is always exquisitely costumed in the first stare of fashion and it is obvious why! Each day she deliberately comes to cajole money from Mr. Allen for some new bonnet or fancy gown that she claims she simply must have."

"And does she get it?"

"Most certainly, and that is what I am trying to tell you. Whoever they are and whatever they want I've never known Mr. Allen to refuse anyone anything."

"I suspect your beautiful blonde is one of those high-flyers," Emma said with a significant giggle. "Of course, we poor innocents must claim to know nothing of their sort or speak anything of them."

"You are very likely on the mark, for she subjects Mr. Allen to the most vulgar familiarities," said Venetia, remembering the day the questionable female had boldly stood behind his stool and rumpled his hair. Though he had not so much as paused in his painting, Venetia had seen him smile, and he had certainly made no protest when that female had extracted a goodly number of notes from the bowl. "I am persuaded she must be his particular light o'love."

"Think you so, really, Venetia?" squeaked Emma. "How scandalous! Of course, unlike Lord Axley, Mr. Allen is not married, so it is not so very bad. I have heard tell that these women of easy virtue have a certain appeal to all sorts of gentlemen and . . ." Emma hesitated, a worried frown creasing her brow. "Oh, Venetia, I should die if my Edward should ever succumb to the charms of such a one."

"But Emma dear, that would never happen, for you and Edward truly love each other."

"Yes," said her friend with a deep sigh. "But my old nurse, who speaks of things of which Mama wouldn't dare whisper, says there is a vast difference between romantic love and connubial bliss."

"Emma!"

"Good heavens, Venetia, you needn't appear so shocked. And you ought not to be such a peagoose about it if you mean to have a happy marriage. Nurse says it is commonly supposed and accepted that husbands take great pleasure in servicing their wives and that their wives are most complacent when their husbands seek more adventurous sport.''

Venetia, whose romantic fancies had never ventured further than between the covers of Mrs. Radcliffe's latest novel, stared blankly at her friend. "Mama has never said anything about... about the marriage bed," she said slowly. "But she did say that husbands cherish a complacent wife."

"Well, I shan't be complacent!" Emma lifted her chin in a gesture of defiance.

"Shan't you?" Venetia asked, a little awed.

"No, indeed! I am determined that Edward need never seek his pleasure elsewhere. I shall myself be his fancy piece!"

"But how can you?" asked Venetia, impressed and deeply interested in spite of her embarrassment. Perhaps if Emma knew about such things and could tell her—

"I fear I am not precisely sure," said Emma, "but Nurse avows that one should always appear enticing so... Oh dear, I shall have to show you." Emma crossed to her walnut armoire and removed a garment that was covered by a bed linen. Turning to face her friend, she stripped off the covering, revealing a negligee so exquisite and so daring that Venetia gasped.

"Oh, Emma," she said, sighing in admiration while reaching to touch the frothy confection of lace and silk. "It's so lovely, so..." *Enticing,* she thought as she lifted a fold to the light. Through the sheer fabric even the lines of her palm were clearly visible. Oh, my! If she were to picture herself alone with Bertram, wearing such a thing. He would see . . . touch . . . Shocking imaginings reverberated through her brain; her heart pounded and her blood grew hot with the thrill of anticipation!

LADY EUGENIA FIELDING swept a triumphant gaze over her crowded ballroom. To think she had been worried that she would not be able to surpass the success of Lady Elton's recent gala, positively garish with all those Turkish draperies and pillows. She had been sceptical when her decorator had recommended the simplicity of flowers and plants. But she had been right to trust him. The ballroom was a paradise of luscious foliage, dotted liberally with colourful blossoms suffusing the air with a thick romantic fragrance made all the more heady by moonglow and hundreds of candles. She made no doubt this ball would be the talk of the Season!

"Eugenia, you have quite outdone yourself!" Lady Axley lifted her glass of champagne in tribute. "Such a squeeze."

"Gracious! Too true, I fear, Frances." Lady Fielding's sigh did not quite conceal her smug satisfaction. The ton had flocked to the ball, strutting about like so many peacocks and peahens on parade. It might be no great social error to be absent from a Fielding ball, but no one would dare snub the Duke of Hazlemere.

"Brace yourself, my dear." The tap of Lady Axley's fan against Eugenia's shoulder signalled the approach of Lord Botley. "The old rattlepate always tries to be first with the latest on-dit!"

This foppish gentleman greeted both ladies effusively before fixing Lady Fielding with an arch expression. "I hear that the hand of your fair daughter has at last been won, my lady. Might I hazard a guess as to which is to be the lucky gentleman amongst the dozens of hopefuls who have been wearing out your door knocker these past weeks?"

But Lady Fielding was not about to spoil her husband's announcement of the secret, however well-known.

"Tosh, my lord, surely you exaggerate! Of course it is true that Venetia has made many friends." *Lord!* How she had wished to turn away all the danglers from their door once she had seen Venetia had fixed the duke's interest. "But dozens of hopefuls?" Eugenia waggled a finger at Lord Botley. "Sir, you must know that my daughter is not a heartless flirt. She would never raise a gentleman's expectations where there was no hope of affection returned!" Lady Fielding bestowed a gracious smile on Lord Botley and turned to ostensibly survey the crowd. She surreptitiously removed her lavender-scented lace handkerchief and patted her nose nervously. Each time she thought back to a certain young Yardley, she began to palpitate. Venetia had taken a fancy to the young upstart, who was only in line for a baronetcy, and had quite set her cap for him. Lady Fielding had not been able to budge her. For Venetia could be as stubborn as a mule and just as obstinate when crossed. Thank heaven, the duke had been besotted with her. "...Lady

Alcorn, how lovely to see you." Eugenia stretched a hand to the dowager in purple satin. "I'm so pleased you could join us on this happy occasion."

Lady Alcorn said she would not have missed the party for the world, Lady Axley enquired after the dowager's granddaughter, and Lord Botley lifted his quizzing glass to peer at a late arrival. Lady Fielding followed his gaze and gasped at the sight of the stunningly attractive woman standing so regally beside her escort, Lord Emerson. Her golden-bronze hair was piled high in an elaborate coiffure, her wide-set hazel eyes insolently searched the room and her lush, full figure was clearly delineated by the close-fitting lines of her gold georgette gown.

"Lady Beatrice!" Lady Fielding exclaimed. "I didn't expect . . . that is, I sent an invitation of course, but I thought . . . dear me, she must have come back to Town earlier than— Pray excuse me," she said in some agitation as she hurried off to greet her guests.

"Her timing is impeccable," remarked Lord Botley drily.

"A trifle late, I would say," the dowager commented with asperity.

"Not too late to cause trouble, I daresay," said Botley, a fiendish glint of gleeful anticipation lighting up his eyes. "Well, well, well . . . I gather she must have received a missive suggesting that she cut short her sojourn on the Continent."

Lady Fielding, now smiling sweetly as she welcomed the countess, pondered the same question. Not that it signified. The banns were to be published tomorrow in the *Gazette*. It was common knowledge that Lady Beatrice's liaison with the duke had lasted longer than most affairs and would likely continue. But even she could not expect him to marry her in the event her goutish husband should conveniently expire! Hazlemere was eager for an heir, and the countess, despite all the artifices employed to preserve her youthful appearance, was almost certainly past her most fertile years.

"Lady Beatrice, how delightful! I had heard you were on the Continent and feared we should be denied the pleasure of your company. But I see that you have returned . . . how fortunate we are!"

"Yes, Lady Fielding. I had been away and returned to London just last night. Though *I* am the fortunate one, for I would hate to miss such a special occasion." Her smile was beatific but her expression was enough to send frissons of alarm up her hostess's neck.

Lady Fielding fluttered her fan anxiously. "I have rarely seen you look so well, your ladyship. Such a youthful bloom on your cheeks. Are we to give the credit to the healthful Italian sun?"

"You are too kind, Lady Fielding," the countess replied with an edge in her voice. "It is true that the Italian sun proves most beneficial. My husband, the earl, could not bear to leave it just yet…his gout, you must know. He intends to join me in Town in a few weeks' time, but Lord Emerson has been so kind as to agree to escort me here this evening."

Lady Fielding exchanged further pleasantries with the couple and beckoned to a passing footman to serve them with caviar and champagne before excusing

herself from their company to mingle with the other
guests.

The eleventh hour marked the long-awaited moment. The orchestra was stilled and a hush fell over the
assemblage as Sir Horace Fielding took his place upon
the raised platform, and stood before them to deliver
the anticipated announcement. Just as anticipated was
the length of his speech, liberally punctuated with
references to his "clever, charming and captivating
little girl," as well as a few pompous remarks about
the duke's consequence and a pointed reference to his
own now that they were nearly related. After having
satisfied himself, Sir Horace delivered his proud
proclamation. "And so, my lords and ladies, tonight,
I have the honour of announcing the bethrothal of my
daughter, Venetia, to His Grace, Duke of Hazlemere."

"Do you look carefully at Eugenia Fielding,"
whispered Lady Gardner to her husband as they
moved towards the happy mother to extend their felicitations. "So puffed up in her own consequence I
fear she will burst like a hot-air balloon. I vow there
will be no bearing her now." Upon having reached
their hostess, Lady Gardner was instantly transformed. "Oh, Eugenia, my dear, such wonderful
news," she gushed. "I do wish Venetia happy!"

"Thank you, Elizabeth," said Lady Fielding. "And
as one mama to another, I hope that I shall be able to
wish the same for your Caroline soon. Such a lovely
girl." As the two ladies lightly embraced, Lady Fielding could not help but feel smug. Caroline Gardner
had set her cap for Hazlemere for two whole Seasons.

Though Eugenia found herself surrounded by well-wishers, she accepted the centre stage as her due. Of course, she applied herself immediately to Her Grace, the Duchess of Whitehead.

"You must be very proud," said the duchess. "And Venetia is such a charming girl. Perhaps you might find the time to visit with us at White Hall before the wedding."

"Why thank you, Your Grace. We should like that above all things!" Lady Fielding fairly crowed aloud with the pleasure of this first invitation from the famous top-lofty harridan. An invitation extended no doubt because she was soon to become mother-in-law to the duke! Well, well...she had always known Venetia's beauty would not be wasted.

She stood in a euphoric haze as the crowd ebbed and flowed about her, offering their congratulations... "an estimable match"..."such consequence"... "charming girl, so nice to see her settled so well." To all of which Lady Fielding murmured, "Thank you, I only wish my daughter to be happy."

And Venetia *was* happy. Happier than she had ever been in her life. Surrounded as they were, she could barely believe that Bertram now stood at her side as her truly betrothed. Though she was especially pleased to share her happiness with friends, even as she received their congratulations, her eyes kept straying to Bertram. Her fiancé, so devilishly handsome in his formal evening attire, standing head and shoulders above the crowd, distinguished by his stature and consequence. But there was no hint of superiority in his grey eyes when he bent towards her and tenderly enquired, "Happy, my love?"

"Yes, oh yes" was all she could reply, her heart so full of joy that she could see naught but him. His smile assured her that he was equally happy, and at his signal, she returned her attention to the throng of well-wishers.

When the musicians struck up the orchestra, the crowd began to disperse, and Bertram led her out for the first waltz. Suddenly she was in his arms, held closer to him than ever she'd been. He was an expert dancer and their steps matched to perfection as he whirled her round and round in a wonderful dizzying fog of joy.

When he led her off the dance floor, Venetia was besieged by gentlemen, all pinks of the ton who wished to be seen with the duke's future duchess. She danced and danced until she was quite out of breath. Venetia looked about for Bertram, hoping that he would fetch her a glass of lemonade. *Goose!* she thought. *You just want to find him so you may be with him.*

But she did not see Bertram anywhere in the crowded ballroom. Quite possibly he had taken to the back garden where several of the guests had retired for the night air. Bertram was ever conscious of his duty as host and strove to see to all his guests' comforts. When they were married and entertained at Lynderly or at the Hazlemere Town house, she would strive to be a perfect hostess, for she knew by his example what he most desired. The heat of the ballroom and press of the crowd were becoming oppressive. Surely she could look for Bertram shortly, but just now she felt the need to have a moment alone to savour her joy.

At one end of the ballroom, just right of the exit to the gardens, was a great stone fireplace. The fireplace was flanked by French doors leading to two small decorative balconies, seldom in use, and at present all but hidden by towering foliage. But when Venetia was a child, the balconies had served as her favourite hiding places, and that was where she stole to now, slipping behind the palms and pulling the French door to behind her. She inhaled a deep breath of the fresh night air, gazed up at the stars and uttered a prayer of thanksgiving for all her recent joy. The balcony had seemed larger when she was small and she had little room to move. She contented herself with leaning upon the railing and heard voices raised below her. She did not wish to listen but could not avoid doing so.

"I will not be silent! I will not! Oh, you have served me such an evil turn!" came a woman's sharp voice. Could this be a lovers' quarrel? thought Venetia.

"No, my love, no. You must not think so."

Venetia froze. But that was Bertram's voice. How could it be so?

"You deliberately waited until I left England and planned the whole thing while I was away—"

"Don't be nonsensical, my sweet. Nothing has changed, my love. Please, do come back inside. We will be missed."

"I don't care a rap if we are!"

Venetia stood quite still, wanting but unable to flee the spot. She covered her ears but still the voices went on and on, tearing her heart apart piece by piece.

"My love, my precious pet," he continued. "I had not been aware of your return to Town. I only received your note this very morning. Surely you must believe that had I known sooner I would not have spared a moment to come to you at once."

"Yes, yes," said the woman. "But what of now, Bertram. What of now?"

"Oh, my love!" he exclaimed, "now we must be more discreet. I must marry, my pet. You know it is imperative that I have an heir. But nothing has altered, I assure you. Do you think my love for you, the ardent passion we have shared for so many years, could ever be diminished by a silly little chit of seventeen! Oh, my love, my precious. It is you and only you whom I shall ever truly love."

There followed a pause punctuated by tears and words of exchanged endearment.

"Come now, my pet," he soothed. "Let me dry those foolish tears. I will come to you tonight. I promise."

The voices faded and they were gone.

But Venetia remained, numb with despair. It was as if her heart had burst and all the joy sluiced away in a river of pain.

CHAPTER THREE

VENETIA WANTED the earth to open up and swallow her. She wanted to scream. She wanted to wrench off the diamond-and-emerald engagement ring she wore and fling it back into Bertram's face. She wanted to rail at him, kick him, beat him and scratch his face until it bled.

She wanted to cry.

But she did none of these things, for Venetia Fielding was a lady. She would not spoil her mother's party, nor would she subject her guests to a dreadful row.

And so Venetia returned to the ballroom, no tears evident in her eyes, and no anguish evident in her radiant smile. If her conversation was too lively, her laughter less restrained, her dancing too vivacious, her high spirits were attributed to the excitement of the occasion. And if her encounters with the duke were marked by lowered lashes and a cool civility, such shyness went unnoticed, for it was considered to be a very natural reaction in a very young lady so newly betrothed.

Only after the last guest had departed did she retire to her chambers. Maggie was chattering like an over-excited magpie until she noticed her mistress's sombre countenance. Knowing better than to ask questions, the maid helped her mistress into bed and swiftly left. Venetia waited until the house was still and dark and only then did she address her anguish.

At first she tried to deny it. Perhaps he had not been her Bertram, but another... After all, she reasoned, she had not actually seen the man.

It did not work. As if she could ever mistake that beloved voice she knew so well, speaking so tenderly and low.

Declaring his love to another!

Determined not to give in easily to her despair, she tried another possible explanation. Perhaps she had not heard aright. She may have misunderstood or even misinterpreted the conversation. So she reviewed what had been said. "I must marry"..."imperative that I have an heir"..."nothing has altered"..."the ardent passion we have shared"... The words were as indelible as her despair and at last she faced the full horror and the truth of what she had heard.

THE NEXT MORNING she arose, exchanging a soggy pillow for a firm determination.

The hour was well past ten, but her parents were still in the breakfast room, revelling in the events of the evening before, savouring the splendour and speculating about the rewards of their social coup.

Her mother beamed up at her. "Down so soon, my love? Ah, yes...the banns. You could not wait to see them for yourself. They are right there in the *Gazette* for all the world to see! Read the notice to her, Horace," she prompted her husband and sighed with a sigh of delight. "You must hear, Venetia. It is so impressive."

"Ah, yes! And very properly phrased," Sir Horace said as he adjusted his quizzing glass and began to read. "Her Grace, the Duchess of Hazlemere, is pleased to announce the betrothal of her only son and heir, Bertram Rutledge, the sixth Duke of Hazlemere, to Venetia—"

"Stop, Papa! I do not wish to hear it!" Venetia felt herself flushed with anger and wished, as she had last night, never to hear the words spoken out loud.

"But of course, my dear," Lady Fielding said indulgently. "And quite right, too. She wants to see it for herself. Give the paper to her, Horace."

Dutifully, her husband held the paper up to his daughter, who shrank back as if from an asp coiled to strike.

"No, thank you, Papa. I don't wish to...that is...I wanted to ask you to..." Early that morning she had penned a note. She worried it now with trembling fingers. "To tell you—"

"Bertram Rutledge, sixth Duke of Hazlemere... to Miss Venetia Fielding, daughter of Sir Horace Fielding of Farsdale and his wife, Lady Eugenia Fielding," finished her mother, who had taken the paper from her husband. "Oh, I shall grow distracted! Did you see Lady Gardner's face when you made the announcement, Horace? Positively green with envy she was. And that horrid little gossip-monger Lord Botley had the effrontery to try to pry the news from me beforehand. But he did not! Oh, such a night! All of Society gathered to hear it first and now the announcement is published and set in stone. Oh, my sweet child—I knew you would land him."

"Mama, please..." Venetia's voice broke on a sob, but her mother barely noticed.

"Ha! The gossips had it that you would never bring him up to scratch! Lady Yardley even told me that they were laying bets at White's. She had it from her cousin, the marquis, and—"

"Stop!" Venetia's voice was so sharp that even her mother looked up. "I am *not* going to marry Bertram."

"Not going to..." Lady Fielding's mouth went slack for a moment before she reviewed the situation and turned a becalming smile onto her daughter. "Don't be nonsensical. Of course you are going to marry him."

Venetia shook her head. She took the note and removed the duke's engagement ring from her finger and laid them both on the table. "Papa, please have these delivered to Ber...to the duke. Or perhaps you should see him yourself to reverse the settlements or..." Again her voice broke. "I must leave it to you to properly end the betrothal!"

"End the bethrothal!" her mother cried as both parents stared aghast at their daughter. "There's no proper way to... Goodness gracious, child, you simply cannot do such a thing! You are officially bethrothed. How could I ever—"

"Eugenia, be quiet," demanded her husband. "Now, Venetia dear, just what are you trying to tell us?"

"I have decided not to marry the duke, Papa," she said firmly.

"That is not a decision for you to make, young lady," he answered carefully.

"Certainly it is not!" cried her mother. "You needn't think you landed him all by yourself, my girl. I was the one who pushed him at you until he came to his senses! And do not dismiss your papa, either. The bills for all the gowns alone cost him a fortune, not to mention—"

"Eugenia!" Sir Horace gestured to his wife to be silent. "Venetia, this is no time to be missish. Now do sit down and tell us what has put this maggoty notion into your head."

"I'm sorry, Papa," Venetia said, remaining standing. She would not expose Bertram for his betrayal even to her parents. She gestured towards the note and ring. "This is between Bertram and myself. You need not become involved."

"Not become involved!" Sir Horace's fist struck the table, causing the dishes to rattle, the diamond ring to bounce.

"Of course we must be involved!" shrieked her mother. "Because of your betrothal, we have for the very first time received an invitation from the Duchess of Whitehead to visit her country estate. And Lady Hansom requests our company for dinner tomorrow evening preceding their grand ball, an honour reserved only for her intimates. And very likely we will be received at Court when you are a duchess! Not become involved! How can you say so!"

"Your mother makes a point, Venetia. You must explain yourself."

"Yes, indeed. Come, do sit down, my dear." Lady Fielding stood and assisted her daughter into a chair. "You're overset," she said soothingly. "Everything has happened so quickly, what with the ball and all. Let me pour you some coffee. No, chocolate is more calming. There, there, my pet. You must tell us all about it. And whatever it is, I'm certain it is no more than a trifling thing."

"Trifling thing! Mama, how can you even think so!" Venetia, whose composure had quite given way, bowed her head and covered her face with her hands. "Bertram doesn't love me," she declared. "He loves another," she sobbed, and the tears began in earnest.

"I knew it! The minute that scandalous Lady Beatrice turned up! Oh!" Lady Fielding exclaimed in exasperation. "Why couldn't she have remained in Italy until after... Now, Venetia, don't take on so. You mustn't believe malicious gossip or any of the horrible on-dits you—"

"On-dits!" Venetia cried. "I heard him myself. I heard him telling her that he loved her. *Only* her and—"

"And what should that signify, for goodness' sake!" Lady Fielding demanded. "It is you he wishes to marry!"

"Only to bear him an heir."

"Quite right, my dear," said her mother. "And there is not a thing to find fault with in that. Wives are very often chosen for that reason and it's an honour to—"

"Honour!" Venetia's head snapped up and her eyes blazed. "He said I was a silly chit of seventeen and—"

"That's just the way of the nobility, my dear. Always they want young wives. Young and fresh and—"

"I am *not* a silly chit! And I'm eighteen!"

"Of course you are not. I mean—yes you are. Dear me, I shall surely take a fit of the vapours! Venetia, I beseech you, do not fly into the boughs over this. I tell you it is a mere nothing!"

"How can you say so, Mama," Venetia argued, "when I heard him say he loved her and refer to the ardent passion they had shared?"

"Venetia, don't be such a wet-goose!" Lady Fielding snapped. "You are innocent as to the ways of the world, which of course is as it should be. But, good Lord, child, if you are to be married you must face the truth," she said sharply. "It is no secret that gentlemen are predisposed to indulge in these . . . these little affairs. It is a wise wife who turns a deaf ear and a blind eye. You must learn to be complacent and— Oh, dear, what have I said!"

For Venetia had stood, her face set in angry resolve. "I shall never marry a man who does not love only me."

"Blast it! This is the outside of enough!" Sir Horace also stood and pointed a finger sternly at his daughter. "Enough of this nonsense about love! Hazlemere's fortune and his title are quite sufficient for you, my girl! His behaviour has been above reproach, and in spite of his considerable consequence he has treated us as family. And now that the banns have been posted, you suggest I repay his generosity by permitting you to cry off! I would not so wound his pride, injure his sensibilities!''

"But what of my sensibilities?''

"The devil take your sensibilities!'' roared her father. "Think of your reputation, my girl. You turn off the duke and you will never be received anywhere ever again. And I tell you that if you are willing to allow his clandestine trysts with a known harpy to keep you from becoming his duchess, I am not! I am your father and I say you *will* marry the duke!''

VERY LATE the following evening, Victor Allen's house at Fitzroy Square was, as usual, ablaze with lights and alive with laughter. Victor's passion for art, literature and music was only exceeded by his passion for people, and his big drawing-room drew like bees to honey all those who shared the same interests. Tonight, Victor sat at his ease among a convivial group, a glass of wine in one hand, while draping his other arm casually around Sally Ellerby, who sat beside him on the sofa. Sally was an exceptionally beautiful blonde who often served as a model for some of his paintings, and with whom he enjoyed a casual and frequently intimate acquaintance. With several of the usual habitués of Victor's parlour, they were listening to Charles Simpson's reading of the latest episodes in his adventures as a foundling boy. Simpson, only one month older than Victor's five and twenty, had been his bosom companion since the eleven-year-old Victor had arrived in London.

Charles had resigned his job at a newspaper to devote all his time to his novel when it had been accepted to run in the *Chronicle*. He accepted Victor's invitation to take up residence with him since his funds would be low for some time.

He's a damn fine writer, Victor thought, finding himself completely absorbed in the tale.

Sally, however, seemed restless and interrupted his thoughts. "I don't like it," she said baldly. "It's too sad!"

Having overheard her comment, Charles felt compelled to answer her back. "But the story is based on the real world, Sally. And well you know it. You ain't that unfamiliar with the streets, my girl," he said smugly.

She sniffed. "Pot's got no cause to call the kettle black!"

"That is not the point. I am simply writing about what I know to be true," he replied reasonably.

"And the Lord knows it *is* the God-given truth! Many's the poor little tykes I've seen just so brutally mistreated!" Jim Turner, the hefty hostler who maintained the big stable off Bond Street, dabbed at his eyes with a fat fist. "Fairly makes me blood boil!"

"Exactly!" cried Sally. "And nobody wants to be made to feel so low. They want to be entertained! Ain't that so, Tisha?" She appealed to the flamboyant young woman seated next to Lord Axley.

Tisha allowed that the story was monstrous sad but then she did like a good cry now and again, and the novel did make you itch to know what happens next... "Don't it, dearie?" She turned adoring eyes to Lord

Axley, who only started and grunted. He had shed his
coat and loosened his cravat and, having consumed
several glasses of Victor's port, had not heard one
word of the reading.

Sally flashed him a look of disgust and appealed to
one of the two young girls seated on the opposite sofa.
"What do you think, Linda? Wouldn't you like
something with a bit of dash and more romantical
like?"

"Oh, la!" The little brunette giggled, but before she
could say more, her sister intervened.

"Plenty o' dash in Charlie's stuff," she said.
"Wait'll you hear what pops up next when—"

"Wasn't asking you, Lucy," Sally interrupted,
contending that everybody knew Lucy was enthralled
with whatever drivel Charles put on paper. A lively
quarrel ensued, to which the author, making copious
notes on his manuscript, paid not the slightest heed.

It was Victor who silenced the hen fight with a firm
"Quiet! Let him finish!" He glanced at Count Laurent. That distinguished grey-haired gentleman was
gazing impassively at the toe of one of his impeccably
polished boots, but Allen could tell that he was listening to the reading. The count would more nearly rep-
resent the audience Simpson aspired to reach. Like
Allen himself, the count had been born to the French
nobility and had escaped the guillotine during the
Revolution by fleeing to England. And, as far as Allen could determine, must have escaped with much of
his wordly goods and fortune, for during all the years
Victor had known him, he had lived very elegantly in
an expensive Town house with a full complement of

servants. If Simpson's tale could touch the count, who had himself never been exposed to such hardships, surely the story would touch anyone, Allen thought. And he meant to hear Laurent's opinion.

As it happened, however, the chance for Simpson to continue his reading was abruptly ended with the late arrival of two more guests. Mr. Elbert Hopkins, who managed the Opera House in Haymarket, and his wife, Isabel. Actually it was Mrs. Hopkins who managed the house, scheduling performances, arranging rehearsals and directing the hired help. Elbert, a virtuoso musician equally skilled with winds and strings, confined his attention to the Opera House orchestra.

The arrival of the tall studious musician and his fat jolly wife was greeted with shouts of joy by the sisters, Linda and Lucy, who had been waiting for Elbert to accompany them on the pianoforte in order that they might perform their comedy of dance and song. Indeed Simpson's manuscript was completely forgotten as the girls instantly seized Elbert and seated him at the pianoforte.

While loath to admit it, Victor enjoyed the girls' song and dance and the temporary respite from Simpson's woeful tale. And, truth to tell, he wished the girls well. They had been rehearsing their comedy for weeks, hoping to be accepted by one of the travelling shows. If they succeeded in this, they had told him in their cocquettish way, he would be relieved of at least two of his non-paying guests.

But personally, Victor imagined such a thing unlikely to happen. To be painfully honest, neither of the girls was particularly fetching or more than passable as a performer. He was pondering their probable disappointment when Jonathan, his manservant, approached him, appearing to have a rather serious problem.

"Sir, you have visitors," he whispered.

"Thank you, Jonathan. Show them in." Late visitors were not unusual at the Allen residence and he took very little notice to the extent that he was unaware that Jonathan had remained. However, when Victor felt a slight tap on his shoulder and read the urgency in Jonathan's expression, he excused himself to follow the servant from the room.

"What the devil are you up to, Jonathan?" he asked as he looked around the wide hall and saw no one. "Where are these 'visitors' you referred to?"

"I saw them into the back parlour, sir. I thought it best."

"Best?" he asked, rather mystified as he followed his man down the hall.

Jonathan did not respond but, having reached the back parlour, opened the door for his master to enter. As Allen moved into the room he stared in astonishment at Miss Venetia Fielding, seated in a straight-back chair, accompanied by her abigail, who stood beside her. On the floor next to the maid were three bandboxes and a portmanteau.

"What the dev...? I mean to say how...why...?" he faltered before remembering his manners. "Good evening, *mademoiselle.*"

"Good evening, Mr. Allen," she answered. "And indeed I am sorry to trouble you at such a late hour. But I didn't...that is, I didn't know where else to go."

CHAPTER FOUR

"PARDON?" Victor stared in stupefaction at the un-expected visitors. Nowhere else to go, had she said? Surely he had not heard aright.

"If you could accommodate us, we should be most grateful, Mr. Allen. Indeed we shall not trouble you for very long." Miss Fielding sat very straight with her hands folded in her lap. She appeared very young, very proper, and very determined. "You will be relieved of our presence as soon as we are able to make other arrangements."

"Arrangements?" Allen croaked. What the devil was she doing here at this hour accompanied only by her abigail...and what of those accursed boxes? "What arrangements?" he asked, his voice almost dissolving into a hoarse whisper.

"If I could speak with you privately." She looked pointedly at Jonathan, whose face reflected Victor's own puzzled curiosity. Reluctantly, Victor dismissed his manservant, who went out followed by Miss Fielding's abigail. Victor felt strangely uncomfort-able, left alone with this child.

"Now, *mademoiselle*. How may I serve you?" he asked as propriety demanded, desperately hoping there would be a simple explanation that would require nothing more of him than returning her to her papa.

"I have left my home, Mr. Allen," Venetia said without preamble.

"Eh?" He gave a start, but then relief immediately followed. He now suspected little more than a family brangle which this privileged child had taken too much to heart. "Come now, *mademoiselle,*" he began softly. "This problem, I apprehend, can be easily remedied. Your poor parents must be frantic with fright. I assure you that as soon as you return they will—"

"I will never return, sir! And may I assure *you* that my parents are not the least bit frantic," she said boldly. "They presume me to have taken to my bed in a fit of pique. At present they are enjoying the company of Lord and Lady Hansom at a pre-ball dinner. A privilege, I might add, reserved only for those with the highest connections." She gave a bitter laugh, which turned into a sob. "Oh, no, Mr. Allen. They will only be frantic when they learn that they may never again be invited to glory in such an honour."

Venetia patted at her nose with a lace handkerchief and quickly regained her composure. But her anguish had not escaped his attention. If her parents had not been the cause of her distress, then who? The answer leapt instantly to his mind. A lovers' quarrel! Yes, at her sittings this was the girl who had glowed with love as she spoke of her betrothed . . . a duke it was. Someone of great consequence, he recalled. Very likely, he thought. A girl so young and so much in love could be hurt by the most trivial incident. He pulled up a chair and took her hands in his.

"My dear girl," he said, "let us discuss this. The course of true love is never without problems, you know. If you've had a quarrel with your beloved—"

Venetia snatched her hands away from his and stood up. "There has been no quarrel, Mr. Allen, and there is nothing to discuss. I have made my decision. Truly, there is no need for you to concern yourself with my affairs!"

"I beg your pardon, *mademoiselle!*" Victor exploded, also standing. "You come here in the middle of the night and simply expect that I should take you in? It is you who has involved me in your *affaires!*"

"I am indeed sorry to have thrust myself upon you at such an hour." The fact that she did not appear the slightest bit remorseful rankled, and he stared fixedly at her, trying to determine what she was playing at. "I'm seeking shelter temporarily only. A few days at most. You see, I find myself in a rather awkward predicament."

Awkward predicament? And she had come to him? "My dear child," he told her, "surely you must realize that you cannot stay here."

"Please, Mr. Allen, do not address me as 'child'! And I do not see a reason why I cannot, as you say, stay here. Your door seems to be open to everyone else!"

"Dear ch...lady, you cannot be serious!" Victor ran a hand distractedly through his hair and, as he often did when greatly perturbed, muttered rapidly to himself in his native tongue. *Confound the silly chit! Be-*

cause of some slight altercation with her parents or her fiancé she takes to her heels and comes here, of all places! Damn, I am not running a blasted hotel, and why could she not have chosen one of the many splendid authentic London hotels, which would have been the sensible thing for a girl of her means and breeding to do? Good Lord! His exasperated utterances were liberally peppered with several choice expressions from the gutters of France. Finally he turned to face her and spoke calmly in English. "Mademoiselle Fielding, you must please listen while I explain—"

But to his surprise, Miss Fielding had indeed been listening and responded to him in fluent French. "That is unnecessary, Monsieur Allen. You have made yourself quite clear," she said.

Victor Allen was much taken aback. Had she then understood *everything?*

She had. Moving quickly, she began to collect her boxes. "It was hardly necessary to address me in such vulgar terms and I—"

"But *mademoiselle,* I was not addressing you!" Damn, how was he to know she could speak and understand French?

"Nevertheless, Mr. Allen, I do appreciate plain speaking. I realize it was a mistake to force ourselves upon you. Pray forgive the intrusion," she said as she moved towards the door. He intercepted her, relieving her of a box.

"Please, Miss Fielding, at least allow me to escort you to your home. Surely, whatever has happened need not require such serious action.

"Do not speak of things about which you know nothing!" she said as she struggled to wrest her box from him. "This was not some trifling altercation but a monumental disaster. And one that can never be put right!"

"Then I must believe you!" he said in exasperation. "But please, dear lady, let me escort you to a respectable hotel. Or," he said with a sudden inspiration, "perhaps the home of a friend. Surely there must be someone you could stay with until . . ."

Miss Fielding's green eyes flashed emerald sparks at him. "Sir, I thought I had also made myself perfectly clear. I have no intention of returning to my home nor do I wish to remain anywhere where my parents might discover me. As they most certainly would were I to take up residence with a friend. Even were I to take a room in a London hotel, there are so few that it would not be difficult to find me. And they are expensive for someone with such limited funds. Oh, bother it!" Thoroughly vexed now, she jerked on the box, dislodging it from his slackened grip. The box toppled to the floor, falling open and spilling its contents. "Now, see what you've done!" she cried, and dropped to her knees to retrieve the items of an intimate nature. "Please, do not bother!" she said to Victor, who had bent down to assist her. "If you would just send my abigail in to me and ask your man to hail a hackney for us, we will be on our way!"

Good Lord! Alone in a hackney! He nervously fingered the garment which he had picked up. "On your way? May I ask where?"

"Does it matter? You will not be plagued, at any rate." She retrieved the silk-and-lace garment from his hand. "We shall do fine if you will only hail us a hackney..." Her voice became muffled as she covered her face with the...pantalettes?

Didn't know where else to go, she had said. A cold chill ran down his spine as he recalled Simpson's recent accounting of the difficulties visited upon his foundling boy cast adrift on the streets of London. The boy was imaginary, but the streets...the difficulties...horrid truths. And for an unprotected female... He glanced down to discover that Miss Fielding must have been considering a similar fate, for she still clung to the garment while her body seemed to tremble all over.

"Here, here, child. You mustn't be frightened." Victor moved closer and once again took her hands in his. The garment fell to the floor, revealing a tear-streaked face, drained of all bravado. He felt an inexplicable urge to cradle her in his arms. Instead, he released one of her hands and retrieved his handkerchief to gently dry her tears. "No need to go into a pucker. We'll sort something out."

"No, I see now that I was mistaken." She tried to stem the flow of tears, and when she spoke the words came haltingly. "I was wrong to...come here. You see, because you are so...k-kind...I thought...but I cannot...impose on your...generous nature...like everyone else."

"Do not speak such nonsense. You were quite right to come to me and I will find some way to help you." But even as he spoke the words, Victor wondered what he could do. This girl was Quality, and he knew well that were she to be discovered in his house her reputation would be ruined. Not only she, but he would be embroiled in the scandal.

"You are too kind. Perhaps if..." She hesitated, seemingly as puzzled as he was about the best course to take. But, after a moment, she lifted her head decisively. "I think it best if you or your man escort myself and Maggie out of London some little distance to an inn where we should not be discovered."

"*Mais, non, mademoiselle.* Did you not tell me you had no money?" He could supply the funds, of course. But how like an innocent to think that she could simply appear at a disreputable inn at this time of night without risking her reputation or... worse!

"Oh, but I do have some jewellery I thought I might sell." She withdrew from her reticule a string of pearls that made his eyes bulge. He knew instantly they were worth a small fortune. "These are mine," she announced. "A gift from my grandmother. I had thought perhaps you could advise me where they could be sold. But for now..." She frowned, gazing at him anxiously. "Do you suppose that the innkeeper might be permitted to retain them until—"

"No, I do not!" he said without hesitation. Appalled at the thought of such exquisitely matched pearls falling into the hands of some greedy innkeeper, he reached for the necklace. "Allow me, *mademoiselle.* I shall see to it for you myself." And he'd make damn sure the necklace was not sold!

"Thank you again, Mr. Allen," she said gratefully. "I am persuaded that would be best. You are ac-

quainted with so many more people and places than I.
You would better know where to make the best sale."
Reaching into her reticule, she held out a few shillings. "Perhaps this would be sufficient to pay for a
night at an inexpensive inn?"

"Oh, *mon Dieu!*" he almost shouted, shaking his
head. Whatever brangle had prompted the cork-
brained notion to quit her home, this bird-witted
goosecap was no more fit to be on her own than she
was to fly!

"Oh, dear, I see..." She hesitated, nervously
twisting one of her red curls around her finger and
looking so much like a lost child that he almost
winced. Then she glanced at the necklace, her expression more hopeful. "Mr. Allen, if you would be so
kind as to advance me a small sum until—"

"Absolutely not!" He spoke so sharply that she
gave an apprehensive start. "You will remain here tonight." Surely by the morrow she would have come to
her senses—if indeed she had any!

"Oh," she uttered in a rush of relief. "I am most
grateful to you. I confess that I should feel ever so
much more comfortable here than at some—" She
broke off, again looking self-conscious as she added,
"But I should not like to discommode you in any way.
Maggie and I shall be comfortable anywhere. We do
not need to take up room."

He stared at her, suddenly struck by his own conscience. Was he worried for her reputation or his own?
Had it not been for the French peasants who opened
their doors to him and his mother, risking not only
their reputations but their very lives, he would not now

be standing where he was deciding the fate of this equally needful child.

"You shall have the best room in my house," he said as he helped her to her feet. Simpson would not mind vacating his room for the night, and after all, it was the largest one. It could easily accommodate a trundle bed for the abigail, at least providing some small measure of respectability.

VENETIA SPENT another sleepless night, and in a strange bed. Although the room was Victor Allen's best, it wasn't what she was used to and it smelled of stale tobacco. Maggie had no problem sleeping on the trundle bed beside her, and was snoring loudly. But that was not the cause of her sleeplessness. Her despair far outweighed such trivial matters and was more devastating than anything she had ever experienced.

Bertram's betrayal. No, she could not call it betrayal, nor could she claim to have been crossed in love. For he had never loved her. He had lied from the very first.

She tossed restlessly on the pillow, too weary to resist her tumbling thoughts. She wished her own love had been a lie, but it had not. She had loved him and she loved him still in spite of the heartache. For what had been such a joy was now an enduring pain deep inside her. If only she could purge it from her, carve it from her soul or will it to dissolve.

Venetia struggled to a sitting position, for she suddenly felt as if she were suffocating. She knew she needed to open a window for fresh air, but in the dark in a strange room, she knew not where it was. Suddenly, the truth struck, and she covered her mouth to muffle the sob. Bertram had not only destroyed her love, but her life. Her home, her family, all lost.

After she took a moment to reflect, her innate honesty prevailed. She had lost nothing. It had been her choice to leave. If her parents had only understood that she could not continue the farce, she might have stayed. But they had not and would quite simply not be persuaded to change.

But Venetia now knew her plight was serious indeed. What would she do? She cast about and landed back at Mrs. Radcliffe's novels. Of course! The author's plucky heroines were forever fleeing from a hateful guardian or to escape marriage to an ogre. Sometimes they took refuge in a convent, but instinctively Venetia knew she would find a life of constant cloister tedious. Besides, what would become of her loyal Maggie who was such a comfort to her? Perhaps when Mr. Allen sold her pearls the funds would be enough for her and Maggie to secure lodgings in a not too fashionable part of Town until Venetia could find employment as a governess or perhaps even an actor on the stage. Venetia was as well qualified for either of these occupations as were the clever girls in Mrs. Radcliffe's novels. She wrote tolerably well, could paint and draw and could converse in three languages, for she had not wasted her time at the academy. Also, at parties as well as at the academy, her talent as a thespian had been well received when she participated in crambo or amateur theatrics. You shall make out very well, she told herself. Her papa would never seek her here at Mr. Allen's house, and once she had the money from the sale of the necklace she and Maggie could... Here she paused, for she had not precisely decided what they could do.

A tremor of foreboding shook her as, wide-eyed, she peered into the darkness, contemplating a bleak and uncertain future. When Mr. Allen had seemed so reluctant to permit her and Maggie to stay and she had been certain she would have to repair to some tawdry inn, she had been truly afraid. She was not unaware of the perils of a young girl alone in such an establishment. Had not several of Mrs. Radcliffe's heroines been sold into a brothel or kept by a lecherous landlord for... But each had triumphed over adversity and had always been rescued by a kind nobleman whom they loved and...

She would think no further! For she knew she could never trust or love another man.

Oh, Bertram, how could you! Venetia turned her head into the pillow and sobbed.

CHAPTER FIVE

"DON'T LIKE to trouble you, old chap," Charles Simpson said when, after a preemptive tap on the door he entered Victor's bedchamber. "But could you let me have the use of your razor? Didn't quite collect all my trappings from my room last night and, er, I shouldn't feel it proper to disturb the present occupants at such an early hour."

"Good God, no!" Victor, jolted awake by this reminder of the events of the past evening, sat bolt upright in his bed. "I mean to say, yes of course, Charles. Help yourself." He gestured towards his wash basin and toilette stand. "Very kind of you not to disturb my...cousin. She is accustomed to sleeping late."

"Oh?" Simpson, who was already mixing Victor's shaving paste, turned to cock an eyebrow at him.

"I believe she is on her way to Bath, and it was no trouble for me to put them up here for the night," Victor improvised.

"No use trying to gammon me," Charles said, pointing at him with the shaving brush, "For one thing I know you ain't got a cousin and for another, there would be no cause for you to hide her even if she were. She's Quality, all right, and you take my advice and get shed of her quick as you can."

Victor, much of the same opinion, watched in silence as Charles lathered his face.

"And don't tell me she ain't Quality. But you know, Victor, ain't it queerish how these Society ladies can't abide being without their abigails. You'd think this one would leave her maid behind, knowing she was going to throw herself into your arms."

"You're way off the mark there, old chap!" Victor swung out of his bed to confront his friend. "I for one do not have your address with the ladies, Charles."

"But you don't need address...not with your looks, which your 'cousin' seems partial to. Now, none of that, Victor!" Charles exclaimed as he threw up a hand to ward off a perceived attack. "I acquit you of any wrongdoings in this case. I know you were as much put out by last night's visitors as I was. What I was going to say is that it strikes me as odd that this sort of thing hasn't happened before."

"What the devil do you mean?"

"Just think, Victor. Your commissions to paint Society debutantes have recently been on the rise, have they not?"

"So what has that to say to anything?"

"I only mean to say that more and more beautiful young ladies are trotting themselves in and out, day after day. And they're romantical, Victor. Especially the young ones." Taking up the razor, Charles concentrated on the small mirror on top of the stand and calmly shaved as he resumed speaking. "Thing is, my boy, you're an uncommon handsome man, though you ain't got a notion of it yourself. Only stands to reason, what with you bein' the only thing they got to look at, they'd fancy themselves bedazzled!''

"Charles Simpson, I am not in the habit—"

"Jings, Victor. Don't play the spitfire with me!" Charles took a cautious step backward and gestured to his friend to calm himself. "'Course I know you ain't no gigolo, but it ain't you. It's them. And it don't surprise me most probably the prettiest one of the bunch tossed everything over to throw her cap at you."

"Throw her cap at me—? See here, Charles Simpson. You're under a gross misapprehension. Miss Fielding was only escaping what she imagines to be a hopeless future, though why she came to me is somewhat of a puzzle."

"Don't puzzle me. You've got the softest heart in Town." Charles wiped the razor clean and laid it aside. "Thing is, Victor, old man, I'm better acquainted with you than most, and if I could have been under a misapprehension...so could many others." He shook his head as he started for the door. "Thanks for the shave. Must be on my way." He paused with his hand on the brass knob. "And, Victor, if I were you, which of course I ain't, I'd get her away as quick as may be afore anybody gets wind that she's ever been here."

That, thought Victor, as the door closed behind his friend, was precisely what he meant to do. He had no doubt that one night's sober reflection would have impressed upon Miss Fielding the advisability of her returning to her home.

HE WAS WRONG. After one night, indeed, after several days of sober reflection, Miss Fielding remained adamant in her foolhardy determination to pursue her chosen course. Her concerns centred only on the sale of the necklace and stage connections to Lancaster, apparently her decided destination. It appeared that her father had long since formed a dislike of Lancaster and the family had no acquaintance there.

Victor managed the situation with such an obstinate young lady as best he could. He informed the stubborn Miss Fielding that she must on no account stray beyond the second floor and begged most earnestly that she would remain principally in her own chamber. Meals would be brought to her on a tray. For himself, he regretted that her identity could not be concealed from members of his household who must have observed her taking the stairs to his garret many times during the preceding month. He did inform them that on no account should they reveal her whereabouts to anyone. In point of fact, he made it known that if they valued their lives, they would pretend they knew nothing of her existence. He then informed the rakish Mr. Simpson, noting that gentleman's gaping mouth at his first glimpse of the ravishing beauty, that if he didn't want to be landed a bunch of fives he'd best stay well clear of Miss Fielding.

"Oh, take a damper," was his reply. "I may be a bit of a blood, but I ain't a damn fool. Unlike some I could mention."

Victor took his meaning. But he was on the horns of a dilemma. Even if he could persuade the girl to return to her home, what possible undamaging account could she give of her whereabouts during the past . . .

Good Lord, two weeks! And he could no more sell her necklace for what he knew would be a mere fraction of its worth than he could bring himself to dislodge the naive little peagoose from his protection, with or without funds.

He was at a stand.

VENETIA STOOD at the dressing table in her room, arranging daffodils in the vases Annie, the scullery maid, had unearthed for her. Venetia had parted with two farthings to send Maggie to the market for their purchase. And indeed, the flowers added a cheery note. Their room was light and airy and not at all crowded since Mr. Simpson had removed his belongings and Maggie had scrubbed and polished. In fact, she was beginning to feel quite comfortable here, Venetia thought as she stepped back to survey her arrangement. Satisfied, she picked up one rose and, dutifully ascertaining that all was clear, took it to the room next to hers. There she placed the flowers on the table by the window. Linda and Lucy would be surprised when they returned. She wished she could do more, for the sisters had been so kind.

Perhaps, Venetia thought as she returned to her own chamber, she ought to purchase more flowers so that Mr. Simpson could enjoy some in his room. Imagine! She'd actually met the "C. Simpson" whose story she and Emma had followed with a passion in the *Chronicle!* She could barely wait to tell her friend that she was privileged to hear advance episodes even as he was writing them. Of course, she could never write anything so clever and important as Mr. Simpson, but it had occurred to her that being so familiar with Mrs. Radcliffe's novels, she might at least try.... Perhaps she'd send Maggie out tomorrow to fetch her a quill pen and paper. Meanwhile, she sat down to study the latest offering from her favourite author.

Venetia had no compunction about spending the few shillings she had in her possession on flowers or ink or the like, for as soon as Mr. Allen sold the necklace...

She looked up from her book and frowned thoughtfully. She hadn't expected that it would take him so long to dispose of the pearls. Still, he must be having difficulty finding a buyer, for there was no doubt he was anxious for her to leave his establishment. He had ceased urging her to return to her own home and she seldom encountered him, but when she did, his harried scowl indicated that he wished her at Jericho. Actually, were it not for that scowl she would be quite comfortable. Surprisingly, she barely missed her former life. It was as if Bertram's betrayal had made fudge of the false and fashionable world of the ton. Her parents she did not miss at all. Nor was that strange, for she had never been close to either of them. She had been at the academy for the past three years, and before that she had been relegated to her governess, Miss Pruitt, who had been very strict and pious. Venetia had been glad when the thornback had taken her leave prior to her own journey to the academy.

She would miss Cyrus, her little brother. He could be a mischief but she loved him. And she would miss Cindy, her little mare, that she would never again ride across the fields of Farsdale, their country estate. She already missed Emma, who would be eager to hear of her adventures thus far. And Bertram. She felt the sharp stab of a heart betrayed and was happy to see Maggie enter with her luncheon tray.

"Just soup and some cold meat and cheese," said Maggie, placing the tray on the table. "But Bella's doing a nice pigeon pie for dinner. You'll like that, Miss Venetia."

"Thank you." Venetia put down her book and smiled at her abigail. "You're such a comfort to me, Maggie. I'm so glad you came with me."

Maggie allowed a good-natured sniff. "Didn't have much choice, did I? With you scampering off like you done I'd a been left with no job, ain't that so?"

"Oh, you." Venetia swallowed the lump in her throat. Maggie had joined the Fielding family as a scullery maid when she was barely more than a child, and they both knew there would have always been a place for her at Farsdale.

"I best be on my way, miss. I promised Bella I'd pluck the pigeons," Maggie said as she hurried out.

Venetia watched her with something akin to envy. Maggie would take her lunch with Annie and Bella, whom Venetia had not yet met. Venetia hated eating alone and was not surprised to find the soup was cold. She sighed as she picked at the unappetizing meal. It was not that Bella was a bad cook, merely a most unimaginative one. But if she could supply her with menus... Really, someone ought to take charge of Mr. Allen's household.

"LAWKS, Venetia! You're a downy one!" Linda cried three days later as Venetia tentatively executed the rollicking dance that she had been rehearsing in secret with the sisters for several weeks. "She's a real frisker, ain't she, Lucy?"

Lucy nodded. "Makes it look as easy as ABC."

"Oh, do you truly think so?" asked Venetia, breathless and flushing with the pleasure of such an approbation. "You really think I might suit?"

"'Deed I do," confirmed Lucy. "Come on then, let's us try it all together."

Venetia did not miss a step as the three went through the entire set-piece, and they ended with much giggling and congratulatory embraces.

"Now we're all right and tight, ain't we?" Linda queried, and Venetia looked anxiously at Lucy.

"No doubt about it," Lucy said firmly. "The auditions begin at two tomorrow afternoon and we'd better get to the Surrey Theatre early."

"You don't think Mr. Allen will object?" Venetia asked.

"Can't object if he don't know nothin' 'bout it. Which he won't. He'll be at his paint pots and will never even notice us gone."

"But I did promise not to leave the premises," Venetia said. She did not like deception.

"You ain't thinkin' of lettin' us down, are you?"

"Well . . ." Venetia hesitated, quite taken aback by Linda's almost frightened expression.

"And after all our trouble to learn you the steps and all," added Lucy.

That much was true, thought Venetia. The sisters had been prodigiously kind and, as far as Venetia could tell, did not stand to gain anything by including her.

Lucy watched Venetia intently and pressed on. "You did say as how the sooner you could leave Victor's protection, the better!"

Venetia nodded. Mr. Allen was clearly as eager for her to leave as she was herself.

"This is your opportunity. Ours, too," Lucy said earnestly. "Victor ain't no pinchpenny and don't never make you feel unwelcome. But ain't none of us payin' for our lodgin' lessen it's Charles, and more'n likely he don't pay no more than a brass farthing 'cause Charles ain't never up in the stirrups. Ain't that so, Linda?" Linda nodded vigorously and Lucy turned back to Venetia. "You can't tell me Victor won't be that pleased to see us all took up with the Surrey's travelling raree!"

"I daresay you're right. And that would be famous, but..." Venetia wondered at Lucy's self-assurance. The sisters had been auditioning for years with no success. Still, she did not like to dampen Lucy's high spirits and only murmured that she hoped she would not be found out.

"Now don't you go cudgeling your brain about that!" Lucy gave her a satisfied nod and began to dig through an overstuffed trunk. "We'll be back afore the cat can lick his ears. And I vow we'll just need long enough to pack our belongings."

Venetia wondered how much stage performers were paid in wages. Would her share enable her to support herself and Maggie?

"Ah, here is just the thing." Lucy stood and shook out a garment of green gauze lavishly embellished with spangles and feathers. "You're about Linda's size, Venetia. Try this on."

"Here, I'll help you," said Linda as she began to unbutton Venetia's dress.

Venetia dutifully slipped off her dress and scrambled into the costume, but she was beginning to feel nervous palpitations. Suppose she couldn't—

"My! Oh, my! You really are a beauty, Venetia!" Linda exclaimed as she stepped back to get a better view.

"And didn't I tell you? We'll get no turn-downs now!" Lucy kept smiling and nodding. "We'll be all the go!"

Venetia couldn't see much of herself in the small mirror, but she felt strangely exposed and was beset by a certain worry. Neither her parents nor anyone she knew ever went near the Surrey even though it was located in London. She'd best wear Maggie's cloak and a heavy veil. "I think it prudent that I not use my own name," she said.

"Good God, never!" shrieked Lucy. "We're billed as the Langley sisters, Linda, Lucy and Lolita. You think I'd let anybody call me Lucinda? May be my given but it ain't gonna make anybody want to see me!"

Venetia was plagued by yet another troublesome thought. She had never before performed in front of strangers. Suppose she came down with fright and couldn't perform in the act. Linda had told her of actors being pelted by eggs or fruit and most anything else by a disappointed audience. She confided some of her fears to Lucy.

"Lord, child, you ain't gonna be no disappointment. I vow them coves will be casting more lures than apples your way... even if you don't move!"

This did not alleviate Venetia's concern. "I'd hate to spoil everything for you," she said. "You see, I've never performed except at school or at parties where I knew everyone and—"

"I've got it. Just the thing. We'll try it on for size on the clan downstairs this evening!"

"What!" Venetia was shocked. "Mr. Allen will never—"

"Know anythin' 'bout it," Lucy declared, again delving into the trunk, producing a false piece of abundant black curls. "You'll cover your red hair with this and we'll all wear masks."

Venetia's doubts could not withstand Lucy's determination. And so it was arranged.

VICTOR'S SUSPICIONS were not immediately aroused.

"I hope you don't mind," Lucy said, interrupting the chess game he was enjoying with the count before the arrival of the other evening guests. She informed him that her cousin had newly arrived from Bath to join in their act. "We're that anxious to see how the three of us go on, so we'd like to show it to you tonight!"

Victor nodded, wishing the pesky girl would go away. He was more concerned that Laurent was trying that bishop's gambit on him again.

"She's resting from her trip so I won't bring her down till Elbert arrives," Lucy continued.

"Damn it!" Victor expostulated. The count had captured his queen while he had been distracted by the wretched chit's prattling!

"Oh, Mr. Allen. But I was so certain that you wouldn't mind," Lucy apologized.

"Confound it, girl, why should I mind! Now be off with you," Victor said, studying the board. He wasn't rolled up yet.

As soon as Elbert arrived late that evening, Lucy informed the company gathered that she and Linda were going up to don their costumes and bring down their cousin.

"Costumes?" Charles enquired, raising an eyebrow. "They ain't never performed in costume afore."

"Maybe that's what the act has been lacking," suggested Tisha.

"Lacks something," said Jim, the hosteler, yawning. "Maybe the cousin will add a little colour."

Not likely, thought Victor as Lolita was presented to them and only bowed her head, unable to speak. Too diffident by half for the stage, he decided. And what an atrocious head of hair. But to give credit where credit was due, she did have a good figure and certainly performed with energy, he thought as the girls executed their set-piece. He watched the cousin with a certain fascination. She was too energetic, as if she was struggling to keep up. Having just arrived, she could not have had much time to learn. Abruptly he sat up, staring intently at the girl. Yes, by gad! She was wearing a wig. And behind the left ear...yes! Only a tiny wisp but unmistakable! A lock of fiery red hair!

Containing his wrath with admirable restraint, he glanced quickly at Lord Axley. He, thank God, was asleep. The count's face bore its usual impassive expression. These were the only members of the ton amongst the present company, and both appeared not to have noticed the silly chit. Still...

As a finale the girls exited with a flourish, and Victor was not surprised when only Lucy and Linda returned to the parlour.

"Lolita's just too exhausted," Lucy said rather airily, sneaking a sheepish glance at Victor before eagerly soliciting opinions of the new piece.

Sally, the beautiful brassy blonde, touched his arm. "Shall we move on to my rooms, Victor? I want you to sample that excellent Madeira."

"Not tonight, Sally. A problem, er, business. I must see to it this minute!" he said, and excusing himself, bolted up the stairs.

He tapped on Venetia's door, and barely waiting for her timid "Enter," flung it wide and confronted her. She had shed that bespangled feathered costume and had removed the ridiculous wig. Her unpinned hair tumbled about her shoulders and she was clad in a dressing gown of pale blue silk.

Venetia, who had been expecting Lucy, gave a start at the sight of Victor. But she made a quick recovery.

"M-Mr. Allen," she faltered, all at once thankful for the enforced habits of the academy. Only ingrained teaching had made her neatly place the costume in her wardrobe immediately. "I—I was expecting Lucy. Did the act take? With her cousin, I mean."

"Oh, do you now! That's doing it a bit too brown, my girl! I'd like to know what you think you're about."

"About?"

"And don't stand there looking the innocent, if you please. Bird-witted you may be, but innocent you ain't! Oh, no, the rig is up, you atrocious little baggage. I expressly forbade you to leave this floor, yet you appeared downstairs in a room full of people, prancing like a—"

"Now, Victor, don't you go cutting up at Venetia!" Lucy, still in her own feathered costume, burst into the room. "Scaring the poor child so she'll be too distraught for the auditions at the Surrrey tomorrow."

"Aha! So that's the lay, is it? You abominable scheming wench!" Victor turned to vent his fury on Lucy. "Let me make one thing abundantly clear, Lucinda. I'll not permit you to use Venetia to add consequence to that drab excuse of an act of yours. You'll just have to find some other cork-brained beauty who's fool enough to fall into your clutches!"

"Oh, Mr. Allen, never say such things!" Venetia touched his arm. He mustn't blame poor Lucy. "Lucy has tried very hard to make me fit to appear on the stage. Truly, she is like a benefactor to me."

He brushed off Venetia's hand and glared at Lucy, who backed away. "Benefactor, eh?"

"That's right, Victor. Me and Linda had been learning her—"

"Kindly leave Linda out of this! She cannot have conceived this nacky notion. She's as addlepated as Venetia. At any rate, I'll deal with you later. Now remove yourself at once!"

Lucy drew herself up. "I may be in your debt, Victor, but Venetia is in my employ, so to speak, and you can't send me away to leave her to your—"

"Oh, can I not? Leave this instant or I'll pitch you out!" He opened the door and pointed. "Go!"

Lucy went.

Victor kicked the door shut and turned a thunderous face upon Venetia. She cringed, feeling her knees grow weak.

"Indeed, M-Mr. Allen," she stuttered. "There is no cause for you to be so out of reason cross."

"Cross? My dear girl, it is a pity that I was reared a gentleman. For it would afford me such pleasure to box your ears, wring your neck and throw you into the street where you richly deserve to be!"

"Oh, you odious, despicable man!" she raged at him, for the vulgar threats had restored her courage. "Did you imagine me unaware? I am persuaded that is precisely what you have long since wished to do."

"Well, I haven't done so," he replied, taken aback.

"No. You have done nothing."

His head snapped back as if he was stung by her words. "I have kept you safely housed for the past—"

"Imprisoned me, you mean."

"Oh? It was my impression that you wished to be concealed," he replied acidly.

"Yes, but only for a day or two," she said earnestly. "Until it was convenient for me to steal away."

"It's still damned inconvenient," he roared. "And why you should appear downstairs and display yourself like some flamboyant bird of paradise is beyond even me!"

"Is it indeed, sir? Then I beg leave to inform you that since you have failed to sell my pearls I am forced to seek some other means of subsistence. And Lucy has been kind enough to instruct me in her occupation and advises me that there is an excellent opportunity to secure employment tomorrow...with a travelling theatre company. I—I am unused to performing before the public and so she thought to put me to the test tonight. And I didn't display myself!" she said defiantly. "I was in disguise!"

Victor appeared struck and stared fixedly at her for some moments before enquiring, "You consider yourself fit for such employment?"

She forced herself to meet his gaze, twisting a red curl round her finger. "I own I'm not precisely skilled. But Lucy says I am fit and she will help and—"

"And did it not occur to you that such an occupation might not be fit for you?"

"What can you mean, sir?"

He proceeded to tell her in detail what he meant, painting a lurid picture of travelling through rough countryside in a broken-down coach in uncouth company, nights sleeping on soiled bed linen in cheap inns frequented by ruffians, until she quailed in horror.

And did she know that the pittance she earned would barely sustain herself, let alone an abigail who would certainly not be allowed to accompany her! And that the audience she drew, much less the company she travelled with, would most certainly not keep to the line! By the time he finished, she was in tears.

"But I must earn my own way. And Lucy says I'm too young to be hired as a governess. What, pray tell, am I to do?"

"Go home, dear child. Go home."

"No. It's impossible. I will never marry Bertram and Papa will order me to."

"Nonsense. Your father cannot force you to marry anyone."

"You don't know Papa!" The tears streamed down her face, and she searched unsuccessfully for a handkerchief.

Victor took one from his waistcoat pocket and gently mopped her tears as he had done on that first night. For some reason this made her cry ever the more. "Do you love Bertram?" he asked.

She nodded. In truth, she had not thought of Bertram for days. But now, more than ever, she missed him dreadfully. It had been so comfortable, being in love and thinking herself loved by such a handsome, gentle man who would take care of her forever and provide her a peaceful and happy life. Now she was forced to wear horrid feathered gowns and— Mr. Allen's arms had suddenly gone round her and she sobbed against his chest.

"Then why not marry him?" he asked softly.

Her head jerked up. "I couldn't. He loves another." Haltingly she poured out the whole story.

Victor found himself less than sympathetic. Confound such naiveté! Didn't the chit know that more often than not this was the case with any marriage? He did not precisely say this, but tried to soften the situation, even suggesting that with loving patience and clever feminine wiles she might soon displace his *chère amie*.

"As if I would stoop to be such a conniving creature!" Venetia stormed vehemently, asserting that she would not live such a lie for one moment and would rather chance the travelling road show than be Bertram's chattel for heirs and her dowry!

Victor knew now that she was in earnest. And, he thought, she made a point. Still...*c'est la vie!* But life would be difficult for one so vulnerable. So honest. And yet so determined.

She was sobbing quietly now and he held her close, wanting to shield and protect her. But how?

"Hush, hush. It is not so very bad," he soothed, stroking her silky hair with a comforting hand, breathing in her floral fragrance, feeling the soft feminine curves of her body through the thin fabric of her gown.

Good God! If he meant to protect her, he'd best get the hell out of her bedchamber!

CHAPTER SIX

VICTOR, AWARE of his rather rude exit, returned to his sitting parlour, an apology on his lips. However, only one guest remained. Count Laurent.

"My pardon for such an interruption," Victor said. "It seemed necessary to attend to something rather important."

"So I apprehend." The count laid aside a copy of the *Spectator*, which he had been perusing, but gave no indication of an immediate departure.

Victor eyed him speculatively. "Care for another game?" he asked.

The count shook his head. "Got something I wish to say to you."

"Oh?" Victor crossed to a pedestal table and lifted the decanter with an enquiring glance at the count. When Laurent again shook his head, Victor poured a brandy for himself, took a seat and regarded his old friend expectantly.

The count picked a bit of lint from his coat sleeve. "Got a high regard for you, my boy. Had a fondness for your mother, you know. She was a great lady."

Victor sipped his wine and nodded. Laurent was obviously in a reminiscent mood.

"She was a sensible woman. No desire to cut a dash. Which she could have easily. Had it all—beauty, birth and breeding. Could have married high a dozen times over." His eyes took on a faraway look. "But she couldn't forget."

"True. But she had a fondness for you, too, *monsieur.*" And might have married him, Victor thought, if her heart had not been buried with her husband, who, thank God, had escaped the guillotine by dying of the influenza, months before the bloody Revolution began.

"But she didn't repine," continued the count. "Madame Elise knew her duty. Parting with her jewels to set up this household and send you up for an education was not the least of it. Didn't push you upon the ton, either. She was not that eager to see you snatched by an heiress." He leaned forward in his chair and regarded Victor intently. "She was the one who nurtured your talent. Said you could afford to make your own life." He spoke so vehemently that Victor drew back a little. "Now you're in a fair way to doing just that. Why you've now chosen to go beyond the line and risk everything, I cannot imagine. I only know your dear mother would have been most disappointed."

"Dash it!" Victor snapped. "Beg pardon, Laurent, but this roundaboutation ain't like you. You are saying what?"

"Awkward sort of business this." The count rubbed his nose with his quizzing glass. "Don't like to meddle in your affairs."

"I daresay," said Victor, unable to remember a time when the count hadn't meddled . . . but with the kindest of intentions. "I pray you, cut line."

"As you will, then." The count retrieved a snuffbox and flipped it open, not looking at Victor. "This new dancer, Victor, is no cousin of Lucy's. Why, she's too uncomfortable by half in all those feathers." He held a pinch of snuff to his nose, inhaled and sneezed. "Can't hide a lady behind a mask, Victor. And you can't keep all that hair under a wig."

"I might have known. You've never been a slowtop." Victor slammed his glass on the table and stood up, feeling rather put upon. "I take it you are under the impression that I lured the lady—"

"Now don't fly into a pucker, my boy. Didn't say you did so with purpose. You cannot be held responsible for the kind of face and fatal charm you were blessed with, which so fascinates the females. And it ain't likely, either, that you'd look a gift horse in the mouth."

"My God!" In exasperation Victor clapped a hand to his forehead. "A pretty fellow you and Charles must think me! Believe me, this awkward affair has nothing to do with me except that the lady in question has embroiled me in an awkward situation by fleeing here in a distempered freak when she found that her erstwhile fiancé was enamoured of another!"

"Odso!" The count had put away his snuff-box and was again massaging his nose with the quizzing glass. "Yes, I ran into Hazlemere the other night at White's and he informed me that his intended was rusticating.

Retired to her country home for a few weeks to recuperate from all the excitement, so to speak.''

"But good Jupiter!" Victor expostulated. "Her parents must know she has absconded!"

"Ain't likely they'd tell that to anyone, especially the duke. Don't want to let a prize like him get away if they can help it." The count contemplated the toe of his shining boot. "Still, they must be searching, hoping to return her to their home without a scandal..."

"You don't imagine Hazlemere suspects...or thought her disappearance unusual?"

"Ha! He intimated it was damned convenient, since his paramour had just returned to London."

"Damned *in*convenient for me," said Victor. "Devil of a coil!"

"Yes, I can see that. But, my dear Victor, proper females should be trained to turn a blind eye to such liaisons. Can she not be reminded that this is the wife's lot and be induced to return to her parents' house?"

"No, she can't," said Victor. "And even were I to insist and take her there bodily, what am I to say? I bring you your daughter, thank you very much, Mr. Fielding. She's only been residing with me for a fortnight."

"Ah, yes. I do see. Most awkward. Difficult to reach a happy solution. But you can't keep her concealed forever." The count cleared his throat. "I presume you...or she...must have some planned procedure?"

Victor gave a rueful smile. "Oh, she has some harebrained notion of making her own way—a governess or, thanks to Lucy, an opera dancer! Damn it, I warned Charles off, but who'd have thought to protect her from Lucy!'' Victor thrust his hands through his hair and gave a helpless shrug. "Dash it, she's a very green girl and I can't bring myself to toss her out.''

"Understandable,'' the count mused.

"If you could see any way out of this coil, Laurent,'' Victor said, unable to conceal his anxiety, "I'd...I'd be most grateful.''

"Let me think on it.'' The count tapped the quizzing glass against his chin. "I do have a sister who resides in the country.''

"Miss Fielding won't accept charity. Not much sense, but pluck to the backbone.''

"Just so. But our Sarah might be persuaded to hire her on as a companion. That's somewhat better than a post as a governess, ain't it?''

"If you could persuade your sister, I would stand Miss Fielding's wages,'' said Victor with inspiration.

"I'll write her a note tonight. Today, that is,'' said the count as he rose to take his leave.

Victor slept better than he had for several nights.

FOUR DAYS LATER Venetia sat at her little table, quill poised over the notebook Maggie had purchased for her two mornings before. In truth, she didn't think she would have liked being an opera dancer. She had felt so exposed in that attire and the feathers had tickled. Writing seemed a more sensible profession and it had been going well...beautiful sweet Lilly in the clutches of her cruel stepfather, determined to wed her to the rich but villainous Count Cortez. But now she frowned, finding herself in a quandary.

"I cannot think how to get her from the dungeon," she said.

"Maybe Sir Humphrey could dig a great hole and rescue her," suggested Linda, who had curled up on the bed and listened in awe to the fascinating tale.

"Don't be nonsensical! A dungeon is too far underground," admonished Venetia.

"Oh. Well then," said Linda, undaunted, "how 'bout a secret passage what Sir Humphrey could climb through and then clasp Lilly in his arms, sayin' 'Fear not, my darling, we will away.' You know, all that sort of thing!"

Now that *was* an idea, admitted Venetia. A secret passage which opened upon the riverbank, and Sir Humphrey could sail over in a slip and... Brightening, she nodded. She was glad of Linda's appreciative company. Of course she had been sorry the sisters had not been recruited to join the travelling thespians. But their efforts had not gone entirely unrewarded. A third woman had been required to play in a pantomine and Lucy had been selected.

"She was that glad to go," Linda had confided. "On account of Victor being out of sorts with her. But, I told her, Victor do get riled up sometimes, but he ain't at all mean-spirited and warn't likely to turn us out. But she said it was a job and anyway, she'd already struck up a promising friendship with the juggler in the company."

Linda, who had become more loquacious since the departure of her dominating sister, had been compla-

cent about the whole matter. She had gone down to
register at some agency for a position as a housemaid
which she thought might be better than being pelted by
a bushel of rotten peaches, which had happened after
one performance.

Registering was a good idea and Venetia would have
done the same except she couldn't dare to hire herself
out in London. Besides, she had exhausted her mea-
gre funds and had no means to do so. But she had been
scanning the newspapers for available positions as a
governess or teacher. Writers, Charles had told her,
might face years of rejections before publication.

And she had to get away! She had thought after that
disastrous night when she had danced... Mr. Allen
had stormed and raged at first, but then had been so
kind. She had been so gratified by this change of attitude that she longed to do something for him, something that would in small measure repay his kindness.

"I know just the thing," she said to Maggie one
night when he was away from home. "We'll tidy up
that garret of his. Straighten things out a bit. He'll be
surprised and so pleased."

They had worked by candlelight and for a very long
time. Never had she seen such dust and clutter! But
when they had finished they were vastly satisfied.
Brushes and charcoal neatly arranged and convenient
to hand, the big table polished and cleared of all that
rubbish, which was now neatly stored in one of the
drawers. Maggie had taken all the trash to the dustbin
downstairs.

The next morning Venetia found that she had underestimated Mr. Allen's surprise and definitely over-

estimated his pleasure when Victor descended the steps in a fury.

"Who the devil has been messing in my room?" he roared. "Jonathan! Present yourself! This instant!"

Venetia, hearing Allen storm at the innocent and greatly astonished manservant, felt it necessary to exonerate him.

"Mr. Allen!" she cried, running into the hall to intercede. "You mustn't blame Jonathan. It wasn't... He didn't... We... that is, I did it."

"You!" He turned on her a look of such blind fury that she felt her knees buckle. "I distinctly forbade you to leave this floor, by God! And you—"

"N-no," she sputtered. "You told me not to go below it."

"And that, my little dim-witted meddlesome vixen, gave you leave to wander aloft and pry into my private possessions?"

She backed away, afraid he might strike out at her. "I did not pry, sir. I just...I thought you'd be pleased."

"Pleased, my eyes! Pleased to have all my belongings scattered to hell and back!"

"Sc-scattered? We...I was arranging them so..." She choked on a sob as she felt her eyes fill with tears. But she was not about to be reduced to tears by this ogre. She lifted her head defiantly. "Oh, you are abominable! You have no cause to scold me so severely when I was just trying to order things for you. You of all people must know everything was in horrible disarray!"

"I know, Miss Fielding, that everything was just as I like it . . . where I could at least find it!"

"Find it?" Venetia laughed crossly. "How could you find anything? Why, you could as well have been looking for buried treasure."

"Buried treasure it was, you empty-headed nitwit! Where the hell did you bury my brushes?"

"Br-brushes?" She stared at him in utter bewilderment. "But surely you saw them." They had cleaned and laid them out so carefully right by his palette.

"Yes, brushes. The ones in that bucket by the table."

"Oh, those!"

"Yes, *mademoiselle,* those. Could you strain your befuddled mind back to where your busy little hands might have placed them?"

"Oh, yes. In the dustbin. I had Maggie carry them down with the rest of the trash."

"Dustbin? You consigned my good brushes to the dustbin?"

"But they weren't. They were all straggly and wispy and—"

"For your edification, my little bird-wit those straggly brushes cost me a fortune!" He pointed a stern finger at her. "Just you understand one thing, miss. If you ever . . . ever come near my garret again I'll bloody well wring your neck! Do you take my meaning?"

"Yes, I fear I do. And I think you are a most ungrateful, odious person. How could I have ever thought you kind! I'm sorry I ever came here!"

"The feeling is returned, my girl. How devoutly I wish you were back in your darling Bertram's arms!"

"Oh, if only I were!" she cried, unable to stem the flow of tears. "He would never threaten me or speak to me in such a vulgar fashion! He treats a lady as she should be treated."

"Well, well!" Victor said smugly. "How glad I am that you finally come to that realization. It may please you to know that I am now working on a scheme that might afford you an opportunity to be returned to the bosom of your beloved, to the satisfaction of both of us! But as of now I am going down to retrieve my brushes from the dustbin and you're going back into your room," he said, giving her a not-too-gentle push, "where I'd advise you to stay if you have no desire to have your ears boxed!" He had turned then and bounded down the stairs, so, given no opportunity to answer in kind, she slammed her door... hard!

Venetia had not caught sight of him since then and she did not wish to. Not even to enquire into the status of her pearl necklace. But there had been an advertisement for a governess position in Kent and she had written a letter stating her qualifications, under a false name, of course. Perhaps she would be contacted in a day or two.

"Seein' as how you got stuck on the secret passage, how's about if Sir Humphrey challenges the wicked count to a duel?" Linda asked, reminding Venetia of her present task.

"Well, I suppose he could—"

"Oh, Miss Venetia! Oh, miss! I'm that sorry," blubbered Maggie, bursting into her room at that very moment. "But I swear I didn't see him. The sneak! Not until I was opening the door and caught a glimpse of him! He must have followed me, Miss Venetia! Oh, I'm that sorry, I am." Maggie stood in the middle of the room wringing her hands.

"Who?" Venetia stood in great agitation. "Papa?"

"No, miss. 'Twas Hudson, your groom." So saying, Maggie explained that Bella had sent her to the market and, absorbed in her selection of produce, she hadn't been paying attention to who else was around. "Oh, Miss Venetia, your pa'll be here right smart!"

"Good gracious! What am I to do? He'll force me to return home!" And she knew now, whatever the cost, that she had to depart. "Quickly, Maggie, we must pack up!" she said, dragging out her portmanteau.

"Oh, Miss Venetia, there'd hardly be time," warned Maggie.

"Then what am I to do?" Venetia desperately paced the room. "I simply will not marry Bertram for anyone or any reason!"

"Well, you couldn't if'n you was already married," said Linda.

"But I'm not."

"But your pa don't know that," Linda declared. "Wait till you see," she said, getting up from the bed and running into her own room. She returned and placed a brass ring on the third finger of Venetia's left hand. "There, now you're married. And all you got to do is say so."

Venetia, awestruck, stared at the ring.

"Oh, Miss Venetia," Maggie protested feebly. "Don't seem right somehows."

"Yes it is. The ring's all right," said Linda. "Belonged to my ma."

"But, Miss Venetia," said Maggie. "you'd be telling a lie."

Venetia was silent. She was reliving those terrible moments on the night of her betrothal party. She had made a resolution that night and she made it again now. She would rather tell a lie than live one.

Papa was heard downstairs remonstrating with Jonathan. "Don't tell me my daughter is not in this house! I have it on good authority that she is and I am not leaving here without her!" And by the time he had brushed past Jonathan and bounded up the stairs to be ushered into her room by a waiting Maggie, Venetia was prepared, albeit trembling a bit, her left hand held behind her back.

But, surprisingly, his manner seemed transformed.

"Venetia, my child," he said in tones more gentle than she had ever heard from him. "Gad, but I'm glad to find you at last. Your mama ... all of us were overset. When Hudson told us ... Oh, my child, you'd never imagine our relief!" He moved to take her in his arms. "Why ever did you run off like that? We were all to pieces!"

"But you said ... that is, my betrothal ..."

"There, there, child. Don't fuss your head about that. We fixed things up right and tight. Had it put about that you were resting at Farsdale. Then your mama and I went right on rubbing elbows with the ton, gadding about to this function or that, just as if we had not a care. But I can tell you now, child, we were that worried. Oh, Venetia, how could you?''

"But the marriage . . . that is, you said . . .''

"Now, child, you mustn't take my scolding so seriously. You know how I am.'' He talked to her in such soothing tones that she could barely believe her papa to be the same man. He continued to assure her that she had been sorely missed and if she would just come home, everyone could be comfortable again and everything would be just as it was. Maggie and Linda looked on in wonder while Venetia became convinced that she would not be forced into doing anything against her will.

"Oh, Papa, I am so very happy. And you will tell Bertram—''

"Now, puss, no need to think about that! We'll go up to Farsdale and come right back and His Grace will never know!'' He glanced about the room. "Ain't no gabble grinders in this place, I trust. A little of the ready should keep them mum enough.''

"Papa, you cannot mean you intend to go through with this?'' She cursed herself for a fool! He was still determined that she marry Bertram! Venetia straightened and drew back from her father, as determined as he.

"Yes indeed, my pet, you will still be a duchess,'' he said. "His Grace don't suspect a thing. Likely you'll find a note from him awaiting you at Farsdale. He's most anxious for your return.''

"Papa, for the last time, I am not going to marry Bertram."

"Of course you are. Do you think I'm going to let you make a fool of yourself and of me, as well?"

Ah, yes, thought Venetia, here was the papa she knew.

"But I cannot," she said quietly, at last displaying the ring. "For you're too late, Papa. I'm already married."

He turned deathly pale, then shook his head, gasping. "You're hoaxing me," he said hopefully.

"Oh no she ain't!" Linda insisted, and then, proving herself quite an actress after all, told a convincing tale of true love conquering all in a flight to Gretna Green. "He truly loved her, sir, and when he saw you were going to force her to marry this cruel duke, he came to her rescue and—"

"Oh, he did, did he?" Sir Horace glared down at the eloquent Linda. "We'll see about that!" He turned from her to shake his fist at Venetia. "You're underage, my girl, and I'll have this union annulled! Good God! I was a fool to let you have your portrait painted by this lecherous libertine! I'll ruin him! Where is he? I'll have his guts for garters!"

He tore out of the room and the girls looked at one another in astonishment.

"I never said it was Victor!" squeaked Linda. "Did I, Maggie? You heard me, and I never even mentioned a name!"

"Oh, good heavens, I must stop him!" Venetia exclaimed as she rushed out after her father. "If Papa finds Mr. Allen, he'll kill him! And Mr. Allen will kill me! Oh, dear Lord, someone will be dreadfully hurt!"

CHAPTER SEVEN

SHE WAS TOO LATE. Papa had found Mr. Allen. Even as she mounted the first step, Venetia could hear her father in the garret above addressing Victor in thunderous tones of denunciation. She must stop him at once! But when she raced up the stairs and flung the door wide she saw that her papa had found Victor alone, evidently in the process of putting a few finishing touches on a portrait. For Allen stood, brush still in hand, his expression a comedic combination of stupefaction and amazement.

"How dare you, you miserable, encroaching cur!" Sir Horace's whole body shook with apoplectic rage and his white-knuckled fist quivered inches from Allen's nose. "So! Hanging out for an heiress, were you! By jove, I'll—"

"No, Papa!" cried Venetia as she ran across the room, trying to pry her father away. "You mustn't. He didn't—"

"Oh, didn't he!" Venetia almost fell as her father shook her off and pointed an accusing finger at her. "I never took you for a stupid girl. He may have gammoned you, but I know the scent of a fortune-hunter! It won't wash, you impudent libertine!" he said, turning again to Allen. "Not one penny of my blunt will you see!"

"But..." Victor's mouth opened and closed ineffectually.

"You can be certain that I'll put an end to this havey-cavey affair! I know how to deal with an unconscionable rake!"

"Sir, I suggest you must be under a sad misapprehension," Allen said as he laid down his brush.

"Indeed you are, Papa. Mr. Allen has been most kind. And he...that is, we are not—"

"You will kindly let *me* deal with this, missy!" Again she was cast off. "I do not believe for one instant that vulgar farradiddle about true love and a flight to the border! I should have known all along this paint-monger was hanging out for a rich wife!"

"Wife?" Allen's head jerked back.

"But not for long!" Sir Horace warned in a menacing voice. "Make no mistake about that. I'll soon have this marriage annulled."

"M-marriage?" Allen, a flicker of suspicion dawning in his eyes, turned to Venetia. She felt herself grow scarlet under that penetrating gaze and again rushed to her father, seizing him by the arm.

"Please, Papa. You must let me explain..." But her words were lost in the torrent of abuse he poured upon her head.

"There is nothing to explain. I understand perfectly and I'll have the law on you, Allen! My daughter is under the age of consent and you have married her out of hand! No doubt you have secreted her here until enough time has passed to render me helpless!

But thanks to her faithful groom, I have found you out. It is not too late to put an end to this misalliance and I'll do so at once. I'm taking her away today and I'll also put an end to this shady business of yours, you miserable excuse for a man! Never again will any respectable lady of Quality be lured to sit for you in this den of iniquity!"

"No, Papa! No. You must listen to me. You *will* listen. It is not true that Mr. Allen married—" But Venetia, who had stepped between them, found herself pulled roughly into Allen's embrace, her voice suddenly muffled as his lips firmly closed upon hers.

"Hush, my sweet. Hush," he murmured, his mouth still hovering over hers. "Your father does not believe that it is love and love alone which has bound us together. And no one, certainly not you, sir," he said, challenging her father, "can tear us asunder!"

Venetia, who had been horrified by her father's accusations, was now stunned into silence by the emotions sweeping through her. She was surprised and touched by Allen's gallantry and a good deal overwhelmed by such a strange flicker of desire engendered by the kisses he bestowed upon her as he murmured endearments. "You have nothing to fear, my love. Your father cannot come between us now."

"Indeed I can!" thundered Sir Horace Fielding. "And part you I will. And see to your ruin, you insufferable lecher!"

"And to your daughter's ruin, as well, I take it?" countered Victor in measured tones.

"Eh?" Sir Horace gave a start as for the first time he was brought to consider the repercussions of his pledge.

Victor smiled silkily. "I am persuaded it is now beyond your power to part us, sir. For this union has been of a fortnight's duration. Would it not be best to bestow your blessing upon us, sir...and," Victor added significantly, "upon any progeny that might, perchance, issue therefrom?"

Victor's clever and forthright speech did nothing to abate Sir Horace Fielding's fury. He seemed to be attempting to speak, but it was as if the words he wished to utter were choking him, and he turned so pale that Venetia feared he would suffer an apoplexy. When he did manage to speak it was in a venomous hiss to his daughter.

"Thankless ungrateful creature! To think I have spawned such a wilful wretch! You left the home where you were lavished with all the comforts and luxuries money could buy to come to this..." His glance about the room spoke volumes. "Turned your back on wealth and consequence to live in this hovel! Oh, you will regret it, my girl! You mark my words, you will regret it. I forbid you to darken my door ever again, for you are no longer a daughter of mine and this union will never have my blessing!"

Venetia, shaken to the core by this unequivocal pronouncement, shuddered. Victor's arm tightened about her before he addressed her father.

"Nevertheless, sir, I would advise you to put a good face on the thing. Havey-cavey though our actions might appear to you, it must be of some comfort to know that we are not embroiled in a scandalous affair, but rather a respectable marriage. I beg to remind you, sir, that your consequence, as well as Venetia's, is at stake.''

Sir Horace recoiled from this piece of common sense as from a blow. "Oh, my God! What am I to tell His Grace!"

"The truth, sir?" Victor suggested smoothly. "That you were unaware that your daughter had fallen hopelessly in love with a ne'er-do-well and had secretly absconded from your home to wed him. That you pray he will forgive the unseemly but understandable behaviour of one caught in the throes of undying love." Victor's mouth twitched. "I daresay His Grace has some knowledge of passions that overrule the mind!"

Venetia saw that her father was now weighing Victor's words most carefully and knew that he was far more concerned for the duke's feelings than for hers.

"It pains me mightily, but doubtless you are right. I'd best tell Bertram as soon as may be." He shook his head in abject agony before he again lifted a wrathful face to Victor. "I'll never forgive you for this, Allen. You have destroyed my daughter's future, and have denied her her rightful place as a duchess in Society!" This thought above all else seemed to plunge him into a helpless rage. Finally, struggling for composure, he declared that though an outward appearance of civility was necessary, neither of them must take it as a sign of approbation. "For your mother and I will never forgive or receive you. And neither you nor any offspring of this dastardly union will ever receive a farthing from me!'' he said, and made a hasty departure.

Venetia watched him go without regret. Gratefully, she lifted her face to Victor. "Oh, Mr. Allen, I do thank you for being so...so..." She faltered, the words dying on her lips. For the man who moments before had treated her with such loving tenderness had thrust her away and was now glaring down at her in the most horrid unloverlike manner possible!

"I implored, begged...demanded!" he said in scathing tones. "I told you it was most imperative that you keep yourself concealed! But you couldn't manage to do that, could you?"

"But I did!" she protested, "Truly. I had no wish to be discovered," she said plaintively as she watched him stride impatiently about the garret.

"One more day, mayhap only a few more hours, and I could have had you safely away!" he said, pounding a fist against his palm.

"But you never told me, sir. You sold the jewels?"

"No, but I had a plan, and I distinctly remember telling you that. If you could have just remained hidden in your room as I asked!"

"I did, Mr. Allen. But when Maggie was at the market she was spotted by Hudson—"

"Who sent your papa posting down here. Don't tell me that even you could not think to take yourself off until he could have been fobbed off!"

"I did think of that, sir, but there wasn't time. He was upon the house in a flash."

"Well then, my girl, you could have simply thrown yourself into your papa's arms and begged him to take you home and restore you to your darling Bertram! You know nothing would have pleased him more."

"My papa came here under false colours," Venetia said angrily. "And as you know, it will never be my wish to marry Bertram."

"So you contrived a romantical tale of true love and a flight to the border complete with a wedding ring and a very handy husband! How convenient for you, my dear!"

Venetia was about to deny this last accusation, but stopped herself. Suddenly she felt very beleaguered. "Oh," she said, stamping her foot. "You are a most odiously volatile person, besides being excessively inconstant! How could you tell Papa one moment that we are living in married bliss and then ring a peal over me in the next! I do not understand you. You could have told him the whole of it was a lie!"

"But of course I could have, my sweet," said Victor, barely in control of his temper. "And what guarantee did I have that you would not fake a fit of the vapours and claim I had played you false? I think not. I'd as lief not be marked as the wicked seducer of a silly chit of a schoolgirl."

"I am *not* a silly chit, and as if I would ever do such a thing! How could you believe . . . ?"

He shrugged. "Anyone who tells one lie will tell another! Best to act the part of a disappointed bridegroom."

"Disappointed?"

"Not a farthing will I get after all my efforts to snag a rich wife," he said with an ironic chuckle.

"Oh. Well, as to that, it shouldn't signify," she said, tossing her head. "For you haven't married me at all. No harm has been done."

"No harm? You can say that, you vixen!" he thundered as he glared down at her. "You are the most unconscionable piece of baggage that ever entered my garret. You have overset my household, cut up my peace, slandered my character and ruined my reputation! And you have the gall to say no harm has been done? I wish to God I had never laid eyes upon you!"

"And how devoutly do I wish the same, sir! For you are a horrid, abominable creature! Oh, to accuse me so unjustly! Slandered your character, indeed. If all the havey-cavey creatures that daily cross your threshold have not laid a blemish on your impeccable character, I fail to see how I could do so. And I must inform you that the deplorable condition of your household renders it impossible for anyone to overset it more than it already is. And since you obviously prefer to live in this ramshackle fashion, I do beg pardon for trying to put it to rights." Venetia paused to take a deep breath before saying in a more controlled voice, "I am indeed grateful for the kind hospitality you have so unwillingly rendered, and if you will kindly sell the jewels as I have been begging you to do for weeks, I will reimburse you for any expenditures and will hastily relieve you of my presence!"

"Indeed you will not!" Victor, who had been listening with awe to this passionate outburst, seized her arm. "You will marry me, my girl!"

Venetia, who had begun to leave, turned to stare at him in amazement. "Surely you can have no desire to marry me!"

"Of course I do not wish to marry you. But I will certainly not allow you to destroy my life's work!"

"Destroy your life's work?"

"Precisely. Do you suppose any well-to-grass gentleman of Quality would allow his wife or daughter to sit for me unless we were well and truly married?"

"But I have no wish to marry you."

"Nevertheless, my girl, marry me you will! You are about to make a respectable if not very estimable match. For we are off to Gretna Green this very day! Before your father gets wind of the fact that you lied!"

CHAPTER EIGHT

"SURELY, MR. ALLEN, you must realize that what you suggest is quite impossible," Venetia said.

"Eh?" was Mr. Allen's absent-minded response. He seemed to be lost in deep cogitation, his gaze and attention focussed somewhere far removed from her.

"I left my home to escape a loveless marriage and I certainly have no intention of plunging myself into a similar union with you," Venetia said quite firmly.

Victor gave her a blank stare. "Haste and secrecy are imperative. We must re-create the exact nature of this flight to Greta Green which was taken a fortnight ago."

Venetia stamped her foot. "Oh, do listen to me! No flight is necessary. I tell you I will not marry you!"

"Instruct your abigail to pack for several days' journey. Best bring her with you," he said as he began to leave the garret.

"Wait! You have not heard a word I've said," Venetia cried as she followed him. "I would rather die than marry you!"

Her words were lost on Allen. He had reached the second-storey landing and was himself instructing Maggie, who had evidently been loitering at the foot of the garret stairs.

"And hurry," he adjured the hapless Maggie as he made a rapid descent to the ground floor. "We leave within the hour."

By the time Venetia reached her own room, Maggie was already dragging out her portmanteau.

"Put that back this instant," Venetia demanded. "There is no need to pack, for we are not going." She stopped. Even if she did not go with Victor to Gretna Green, now there was no question that she and Maggie would have to leave. "On second thought, do pack, Maggie," she reinstructed. "We must find ourselves another situation as soon as may be."

"Oh, la!" said Linda, who had been watching her anxiously. "Was Victor in that much of a rage? Oh, I am sorry, Venetia. But it weren't my fault, were it?"

"No, of course not, Linda. Yet I must think what to do." But her brain seemed to be all amuddle. She shook her head as if to clear it. Her first thought was that she had no funds at all. Victor had not sold her pearls and she had exhausted the few shillings she had had left. Perhaps she ought to accompany Victor to Gretna Green, and on the way she would attempt to convince him of the grave mistake he was making. Certain he would come about, she would then apply to him once again to sell the necklace. This time perhaps she would win him over, for he had stated most emphatically that he had no more wish to marry her than she did him!

"BUT SURELY you have no wish to marry this wench?" Count Laurent enquired of Victor. The count had come bearing a letter from his sister, imparting the sad news that she had already hired a companion with whom she was well satisfied. When Victor replied that it was too late anyway and apprised him of the latest developments, Laurent was quite shocked. "Really, my boy, is such a drastic step necessary?"

"Quite," said Victor, who was searching through his desk drawer. "Fat's in the fire. Her father thinks we were buckled two weeks ago. Help yourself to brandy, Laurent," Victor suggested, nodding towards the decanter as he continued to shuffle through papers.

"But it's all a hum," the count said as he poured himself a large quantity of the liquor. "You are not buckled. And you have informed me many times that you had no wish to be leg-shackled."

"Just as you have asserted equally as often that it would be a good thing if I were!" Victor said with a grin. "Ah, here it is," he said, stuffing papers back into the drawer and holding up a bank draught. "Commission from Sutcliffe for his daughter's portrait. Thought I had mislaid it," he said as he pulled the bell rope.

Laurent seemed to be meditating as he sipped his brandy. "Yes, it has long been my opinion that a good marriage might have a steadying influence upon you. But, good Lord, my boy, from all I hear of this hoydenish damsel, attachment to her might have the opposite effect. You must not allow her to apply pressure on you."

"No fear of that. She don't want the marriage any more than I do."

"Ah, well," said the count, brightening. "Then there is really no need for it. I admit that I intimated your income might be affected by such a scandal. But now that I've thought on it, your remarkable talents as a portrait painter would far outweigh any blot on your moral character. In fact, it seems to enhance the artist's popularity. The more havey-cavey the fellow and the larger his appetite for the flesh, the greater his consequence. Why, just look at Lord Byron! Yes, indeed," he said, nodding vigorously. "I am convinced you would come to no harm by a touch of scandal."

"Perhaps not," said Victor, seizing the brandy decanter. "But Miss Fielding would." He poured the liquid into a glass and studied it thoughtfully. "She is so very young, and dreadfully inexperienced. She has been denounced, disinherited and severed from all connections with her family and former life. If she is not married to me, her future is too grim to consider. I cannot in all conscience allow her to suffer so."

"Ah, here you are, Jonathan," he said as his manservant entered. "Will you deposit this draught and draw out some notes from the bank? Two hundred pounds should do. And, oh, yes, stop at Turner's to hire a post chaise and—"

"No need for that," broke in Laurent, who had been studying Victor with deep concentration. "If you are determined to go through with it, my travelling chaise is at your disposal."

"No, I CANNOT PROCURE a reference for you," Victor repeated for the tenth time as the count's luxurious travelling coach proceeded towards Scotland. "I am unacquainted with anyone who would render such a service, even could I assure him of your excellent capabilities as a housekeeper—of which," he added as his mouth twitched, "I am rather uncertain."

"Well, you needn't be, for I assure you I am quite capable. Mama taught me that it was the first duty of any lady to see to the smooth operation of her lord's household, and I am well versed in that regard. I know the number of servants required to staff a household, dependent upon its size, of course, and the relative position of each. I know how to issue instructions and how to plan menus and how much money to allot for marketing and how much to the penny each footman or abigail is to receive."

"I daresay."

Venetia stiffened, for there had been a quaver of amusement in his voice. "But that is quite true, isn't it, Maggie?" She appealed to her abigail, who sat on the opposite seat, facing them.

"Indeed, sir, Miss Venetia was taught all that, for her ma meant to fix her with a duke or earl, and so she showed her how to go on."

"I see. Then it is indeed a pity that we have neither a source for reference nor anyone at present in need of a housekeeper."

"But you could write a reference, and if we consulted the registry at Leeds to look for an available position..."

Victor yawned. "A waste of time, my girl. We'd be as unlikely to discover an available position as we would to find anyone who would consider a recommendation from me to be suitable. If indeed they would risk hiring a housekeeper of your tender years. Best settle for me, my child."

This speech gave her pause and Venetia was silent for a few miles. Then another idea possessed her. Without hesitation, she suggested that Mr. Allen could hire her on as his own housekeeper, for he was certainly in need of one.

"I'm sorry, my dear. It will not serve," he answered. "It has already been put about that you are my wife, and for the sake of both our reputations it is necessary to support the lie. Housekeeping does not fall under a wife's duties as such. So pray content yourself that we will be wed and do, I beg you, cease this useless chatter, for I am exceedingly weary of it!" So saying, he pulled his hat over his eyes and went promptly to sleep.

By the time they reached Leeds Venetia was at her wits' end, for Victor had not been moved by any of her arguments. She was very discouraged and very tired and she viewed with some misgiving the inn before which the coach had stopped, hoping its accommodations would prove more comfortable than the others.

Victor also viewed the inn with misgiving. During the journey, in order to maintain the secrecy the situation demanded, he had purposely avoided all the better posting stations frequented by the Quality. However, he found that the inns he was forced to patronize, besides being most uncomfortable, had, if any, only the poorest accommodations for Count Laurent's grooms and horses. Often he had to seek accommodations for them at the better hostels.

Victor was unused to travelling and had little knowledge of expenses required on such a journey, and the double accommodations had been an extra burden. He had stopped at a reputable merchant store early in the day to draw on his letter of credit for more funds and was told to apply again later that day. He would leave Venetia at lunch with her abigail while he went back to the store before the closing of the day's business. He was distressed to find that the inn provided no private parlour, but since the coffee-room was vacant except for one rather old scholarly-looking man, he thought they could be comfortable enough. Victor seated Venetia and Maggie at a table and assured them that he would be back within the hour.

In helpless agitation, Venetia watched him depart. She knew she ought to attempt an escape but knew just as well that to do so would be foolish. *Foolish.* No one could ever have been more fool than she! Venetia stared at the plate of cold mutton and boiled potatoes, and suddenly burst into tears. If only she had never left her home at all!

Maggie, who had been hungrily devouring her mutton, tried to comfort her. "Oh, Miss Venetia, don't take on so!"

"I'm sorry," Venetia said with difficulty. "It's just...oh, what ever am I to do?"

"There, now, dearie! Things are never as bad as they seem," said a strange voice. Venetia, who had covered her face with her hands, had been unaware that other guests had entered the coffee-room. Hearing the chair beside her scrape, she reached for her handkerchief and turned to see that a woman was seating herself and bending confidingly towards her. She seemed to be a woman of middle years, was rather stout and very lavishly dressed. "Perhaps I can help you, my child."

"Oh, no, ma'am, you can't." Venetia, reluctant to confide in a stranger, hastily dabbed at her eyes. "I do th-thank you but it's all my...a situation I have got myself into. I—I shall be right in a trice."

"I see. But, as I say, nothing's as bad as it seems and sometimes another point of view can put a different light on the situation." The woman gave Venetia's hand a pat. "Now you mustn't hesitate to confide in old Harriet. Oh, do forgive my abominable manners. I'm Lady Harriet Davenport, and I've got three daughters of my own, as you can see," she said, gesturing towards a table where three young ladies giggled and talked with one another over their teacups. "I know how a tender young thing like you can imagine only the worst. But do you just go right ahead and try me and see if I can't set you right."

"Thank you, my lady, but truly I don't see how you could."

"Now you don't know that, do you?" Lady Davenport smiled, and Venetia, noticing that her blue eyes were very alert and very kind, warmed towards her. "Tell me, lovey, are you possibly on your way to Gretna Green?"

"Yes," Venetia gasped. "But how did you know!"

"This is the route, and many a young thing regrets her hasty action." The woman looked around. "Are you being forced into this dastardly deed, my child?"

"Oh, no...well, yes, but you mustn't think that Mr. Allen..." Venetia, in an attempt to vindicate Mr. Allen, found herself revealing at least part of her story. She told Lady Davenport that unusual circumstances had forced her to reside with a gentleman for more than a fortnight and that he now felt it incumbent upon himself to wed her.

"And have you no guardian or relative to whom you could apply?"

"No, I am quite alone," said Venetia, the tears again springing to her eyes.

The lady's eyes brightened, but no one noticed. "Oh, you poor child," she murmured. "Is there no other course?"

Venetia shook her head. "Mr. Allen cannot be persuaded to deviate, even though I have assured him that I am very capable to take on a position as a governess or housekeeper. I am well suited to either, you see."

"Ah!" Lady Davenport's brows lifted. "A housekeeper? And you say you are trained?"

"Yes, my lady, indeed I am. Do you know of anyone who might...?"

"Dear me, the Lord moves in a mysterious way his wonders to perform," said the lady in pious tones. "I have for these many weeks been searching for just such a person. I have quite a large household and my housekeeper had to leave me several weeks ago to attend to an invalid aunt. My, my, this is providential! You are sure you are well qualified?"

Venetia nodded and Maggie hastily corroborated her qualifications.

Before Venetia knew what she was about, and to her grateful relief, Lady Davenport hired her on the spot. Indeed she was rather young and without references, but the good lady assured her that she could tell an honest face when she saw one. She also opined that if Venetia thought her gentleman might object to her new position, perhaps they'd best depart before his return. She added that Venetia ought to leave the chivalrous gentleman a note advising him of her wonderful windfall and new employer, Lady Davenport, which she felt would do much to comfort him. Venetia was in raptures until Lady Davenport rejected her request to bring along Maggie. It seemed there was no room in the carriage for her. Nevertheless, Lady Davenport restored Venetia's spirits by promising her that she could send for Maggie later, for her household was also in need of an upstairs maid.

Quite satisfied, Venetia embraced Maggie, and with assurances that she would send for her soon, gathered up her reticule, bonnet and gloves and was immediately hustled out of the inn by Lady Davenport and her three daughters.

ONE HOUR LATER Victor returned to the inn to be greeted effusively by Maggie.

"Oh, Mr. Allen, you'll never guess. 'Twas the most wonderful thing. Miss Venetia has found a position!"

"Good God!" Victor exclaimed as he felt his stomach muscles contract. "Do not say some amateur theatrical group wooed her away!"

"Oh, no, sir. Miss Venetia met up right here with the nicest most respectable lady what was even royalty. She introduced herself, too, her bein' so fine, and turns out she was Lady Harriet Davenport who had come with her three daughters. The lady said it was the Lord's blessing that they should meet, what with her needing a housekeeper these many weeks. And she weren't bothered that Miss Venetia was young and didn't have no references, on account of she said she could tell right off our Miss Venetia was that honest. And in a trice they were gone off in her carriage and—"

"Stop, right there!," said Victor, hoping he had not heard aright. "Are you saying that Venetia went off with some old harpy without so much as a by-your-leave?"

"Yes, sir. I mean, no, sir. That is, she warn't no harpy. The lady was that nice and well spoken and dressed fine."

"I don't give a damn what she was wearing!" Victor exploded, resisting an impulse to shake the abigail. "You let your silly chit of a mistress run off with just the clothes on her back!" For he knew that except for her small bag of toiletries, Venetia's clothes were packed in her portmanteau on top of his chaise.

"Lady Davenport said as how it didn't matter because she'd provide Miss Venetia with clothes until I got there. See, there weren't room in the carriage for me, but didn't that nice lady leave me three whole pounds!" Maggie's eyes sparkled with delight. "And Miss Venetia is going to send for me as soon as may be on account of her ladyship is in need of an upstairs maid as well as a housekeeper.''

Victor stared at her. ''You're as huge a peagoose as Venetia, and I should have known better than to leave you two alone!''

''Why, Mr. Allen, why are you lookin' like that? Miss Venetia was so sure you'd be pleased on account of she knew you didn't want to be married, neither. And if you knew she had a good position and all you could—''

''Oh, close your yap and tell me how long they've been gone and what direction the carriage took. That is, if you had enough sense to even notice!''

''But, sir, I can tell ya it's all right. Miss Venetia probably told you her direction in this here note,'' Maggie insisted.

But Victor, paying her no heed, was thoughtfully perusing the note Venetia had left for him, and was alarmed but not surprised to see that Venetia had not in fact left her direction, for she hadn't known it.

His mind worked frantically and concluded Miss Fielding had stepped into yet another coil.

Was it too late? How was he to find her, let alone catch up to the foolish little chit? Little did she know the danger she was in for her ''Lady Davenport'' had just recruited a prime piece of baggage!

CHAPTER NINE

LADY HARRIET DAVENPORT sat languidly facing front in her well-upholstered travelling coach. Venetia sat primly beside her. The three "daughters" were squeezed together on the seat opposite, facing them, and Venetia was most discomfitted by their intense scrutiny.

Little was said or could be heard as they rattled over the bumpy dirt road that led to the turnpike. When they reached the toll gate at the entry, Lady Davenport was greeted with great familiarity by the gatekeeper.

"I see ye found yerself a fine 'un this trip," he said as he peered in the coach. "Fetch you a pretty penny, eh?"

"Be off with ye!" was the quick reply as Lady Davenport thrust a pound note into his hand. Lady Davenport waved on the coachman, who sprung the team into a gallop. The jolt stopped Venetia in midsentence but when she regained her composure, she turned to her new employer.

"Lady Davenport, I take it that you and your daughters make this trip quite often."

"We do," the lady said in a voice which brooked no further questions.

But Venetia persevered. "Whatever did he mean, speaking to a lady in that manner?" She hesitated and did not ask what he'd meant by "fetch you a pretty penny." How did that signify? Lady Davenport had said nothing about being in trade.

The coach, speeding through a winding curve, lurched precariously, barely avoiding a collision as it passed an ox-driven dray. Further conversation ceased, since all aboard were virtually flung from their seats.

As the coach righted itself, Lady Davenport straightened her Caledonian cap and called out to her coachman through the hatch in the unmistakable cockney of Lime Street, "Blimey, you blooming buffle-head! Stop making like a jarvey afore you croak us all!"

"Aye, ma'am," he said as he reined the team of four bone-setters into a gentle canter.

Passenger peace restored, Venetia returned to her quandary. She was even more confused and unable to subdue a tremor of apprehension. Lady Davenport's outburst suggested strongly that she was no lady. With some trepidation Venetia watched as her new employer slipped into a more genteel demeanour and addressed all the occupants about "the hazards of travel in these days of breakneck speed."

Her comments were met with dutiful approval by all, and as the coach had settled into an even pace, Lady Davenport announced she would take a nap and was not, she said with a significant glance at Venetia, to be disturbed by mindless chatter.

The admonition was unnecessary, for at the moment Venetia was stricken into silence by a terrible notion growing ever more daunting. She looked across at the three girls, who, she decided, were all very pretty with the sort of rosy complexions many women tried to achieve with paint pots. They all wore fashionable, if not flamboyant costumes much in the same vein as Lady Davenport. Venetia, hoping they could enlighten her as to her situation, began to speak, but the girl in the middle put a finger to her lips and shook her head. She appeared to be the youngest daughter but the prettiest, with an abundance of guinea curls and mischievous blue eyes. Reaching across to where Lady Davenport slumbered, she plucked a feather from her cap and laid it gently on the lady's protruding and slightly open mouth. All three girls convulsed into quiet giggles as the feather rose and fell with each snore.

Venetia might have been amused by the comedic spectacle had she not been plagued by an as yet unconfirmed apprehension and a growing confusion about the audacity of the girls. Again, she started to speak but they were beforehand, simultaneously whispering questions and chattering.

"What's your name, ducks?"

"Lordy, all the gents'll go mad over that beautiful hair.... Yours, is it? Not dyed? Well, ain't you the lucky one!"

"You ain't got a prayer now, Melissa!"

Venetia, also whispering, attempted to answer the questions. She advised them, however, that Lady

Davenport had hired her as housekeeper and her looks were of no moment.

"Housekeeper?" snorted the eldest. "Blimey! Is that wot the old fleabag told ya?"

Fleabag. What sort of daughter was this? But before Venetia could absorb this latest shock, the girls gladly shared confidences that confirmed Venetia's worst suspicions and sent cold shivers down her spine. Lady Davenport owned and operated a brothel just outside Newcastle and all three girls were in her employ, which, they gleefully told her, she was, too, now.

Venetia's hands were damp and she could barely breathe. Though she continued to stare at them, she was no longer listening to these women who seemed to be perfectly satisfied with a fate far worse than any she could imagine. For Venetia knew all about life in a brothel from reading Mrs. Radcliffe's novels. Always the most innocent had been duped but always she was rescued. Who would rescue her?

For a moment, her spirits raised to dizzying heights. Of course, Mr. Allen. But immediately her hopes were dashed. Victor would be relieved by the information in her note, and released from the charge of her, he would be happily on his way back to London.

There was Maggie. Surely, if she did not send for Maggie as arranged, her loyal maid would send up a hue and cry. But would anyone respond, and with no direction? What could they do?

And by that time... A shudder ran through her body at the very idea. Her mouth was bone dry and her throat was tight. She felt faint as a wave of panic swept over her. She must have air! She must escape!

Blindly, Venetia reached for the handle on the coach door.

A firm hand gripped her wrist. "Oh, no, dearie! You might break your pretty neck. And we wouldn't like that, would we?"

With a gasp, Venetia turned to see Lady Davenport fixing her with a piercing gaze that was anything but kind.

"How dare you?" Venetia said hoarsely. "You tricked me."

"So, my girls have been gabbing, have they?" She grunted and cackled, much amused, giving up all pretence of gentility. "Oh well, thought they'd spill the soup sooner or later. No use gettin' into a pucker, lovey. Old Harriet'd have to have windmills in the attic to waste such a pretty piece as you on chores! Ain't that right, girlies?"

The girls, who had all returned to their usual state of obedience, nodded in concert.

"Old Harriet treats you good, don't she, girlies?"

They nodded with exaggerated vigour.

"I'm gonna treat you good, too, dearie," she said emphatically. "So don't you fret none. All you gotta do is please the gents."

"But I couldn't do that," Venetia said, appalled. "Truly I couldn't. Aside from anything else . . . I am without experience, so to speak."

"Easy as ABC, dearie. Just dish out a little Spanish coin and cuddle up a mite and . . . oh, never trouble your pretty little head about that. Old Harriet'll show you how to go on!" She gave a smirk of satisfaction. "Wouldn't surprise me none if some fine gent took a right fancy to you. And he might set you up in a snug little love-nest of your own, and o'course there'd be a little something for me in it, too!''

"Never!" Venetia drew herself up straight. "Madam, you may as well understand that never will I—"

"Don't give me none of your sauce, missy!" Harriet's voice was sharp and she turned a venomous scowl on Venetia. "I've had just about enough of your whinin'! Done you a favour, didn't I? All alone you were, and about to be forced into marrying some old cadger."

"How dare you! Mr. Allen was a gentleman and too kind..." Venetia's voice broke as the image of Victor's face swam before her eyes.

"Ya shoulda thought o' that before, ducks," the old harridan hooted, " 'cause it's too late now!''

Venetia sank further and further into despair as the coach rolled inexorably on towards her doom.

Barely an hour had passed before an increase in traffic caused the coachman to slow their pace. Coachmen on the road often exchanged conversation in a language peculiar to their service. Now, Venetia was able to decipher that they were travelling close to the Ouse River toll gate and the local inn. She wondered if they would change horses at the inn and if so, could she manage to escape?

At the toll gate Harriet was greeted by the gate-keeper, again with words of familiarity. He told her someone waiting at the inn would be glad to see her. Venetia's spirits lifted a trifle as the lady ordered the coach to proceed towards the inn. Surely if there was a crowd...

The inn was indeed busy. The Royal Mail coach guard was blowing his yard of tin, blaring a warning for other coaches to make way. In the yard were two stages, one coming, another going, trade wagons, ostlers, stable-boys and horses. The noise was at a deafening pitch throughout the bustling scene. Harriet barked orders at her coachman to go to the rear of the large two-storey Tudor structure. The driver, something of a whipster, expertly rounded the inn and backed the vehicle into a space reserved for Lady Davenport. Harriet squeezed herself out of the carriage first and nodded her approval to her coachmen. After waiting for the four girls to step down, and taking a firm grip on Venetia's arm, she hustled them towards the entrance like a mother hen with her chicks.

"Got your place all ready fur ya, Harriet," greeted the doorman. One of the waiters led them through the crowded taproom to what seemed to be Harriet's own private parlour. Much to Venetia's surprise, the door to the parlour was left open because the waiter knew that Harriet "liked to keep an eye out for the nobs what were comin' and goin'."

So, although they were in a separate parlour, it was not at all private. They may as well have been right in the nearby crowded taproom. One could hardly hear oneself speak over the shouts and barks and bawdy remarks of those who were foxed.

Venetia was frightened and appalled. Harriet and her three soiled doves were obviously quite accustomed to the situation. A barmaid hastily entered and hustled over to Harriet's table, advising her that a Mr. Muldoon would see her shortly and in the meantime she would be pleased to take their orders. As the three girls chatted, Venetia buried her face in her hands and softly sobbed. Harriet was visibly annoyed by Venetia's behaviour.

"Stop being such a milksop! You was the one wot told me that Canterbury tale and I believed it. So wot if I told ya a clanker. Just paid ya back in your own coin. So stop that bloomin' snivelling and tuck in," the harridan ordered as steaming plates of choice dishes were set before them. "You're gonna need your strength."

Harriet and the girls began to eat with great appetite, but Venetia could not force down a morsel. How could she have thought to make her escape here? Even if she could bring herself to seek help from any of the vulgar persons thus far encountered, she would probably be delivered straight back to Harriet, who, it was obvious, was on home turf at this place.

They had only just been served when Henry Muldoon, the brandy-faced rotund bear of an innkeeper, appeared. He greeted Harriet with an overly familiar embrace, saying, "Sit ye down, me lass," and loudly kissed the three girls. His beady eyes wandered over Venetia, then back to Harriet. "And what have we here, Harriet, me darlin'? Wouldn't be one of them Quality lasses, would it? Are you come new to our old Harriet, me girl?" he asked Venetia, who cringed.

Harriet answered for her. "Picked her up on the road, I did. She's a green girl, but not for long."

"Well, old girl," hooted Henry, "you will save her for me, won't ya? I'll be a-payin' a visit in a day or two. And dinna ye fret. I ain't no clutch-fist!"

They both laughed as he gently pinched Venetia's tear-streaked cheek. "Me and Harriet are thick as inkle weavers, since I were a young sailor and she the sweetest doxy on the dock! And we stayed thick as glue whilst I was a mason, and Lord knows wot all else till the bones did right by me and I went and bought this inn. Come up in the world, ain't we, Harriet, me darlin'?" he said proudly as that lady, never pausing in the consumption of her dinner and drink, nodded in agreement.

Venetia was now in the deepest depths of despair. She had seen her despoiler and knew it was only a matter of a day or two before her fate was sealed. She would rather die.

Death indeed was becoming an attractive alternative, Venetia thought. All she had ever wanted was to marry a man who loved her and she him. She did not wish to be a burden on a good and kind man, much less cause him to enter a loveless marriage for her sake. But must she consider death because she had held to her principles? Yet surely a quick death would be less painless than the one old Harriet had planned for her.

I will not shed another tear! I will escape! Or break my neck in the trying just as Harriet warned me earlier! With her choices resolved she raised her eyes to note a commotion by the parlour door. She heard a great deal of pushing and a muffled French epithet that made her blush. The same voice spoke loudly in English. "I am searching for a lady and I will not leave these premises until I find her!" A lackey who was insisting that this was a private parlour was shoved aside, and in the doorway stood Victor Allen!

Venetia leapt to her feet and ran across the room in a most unladylike fashion to fling herself at Victor with such vigour that she almost knocked him to the floor. Righting them both, he held her close. He had no choice, for Venetia, contrary to her determination not to shed another tear, had grasped Victor in a vise-like grip and was sobbing out her heart. Blubbering and gasping, she managed to tell him of her horrible predicament, eagerly admitting that she had been a complete idiot and was never so glad to see anyone in her life. She concluded with fresh hysterics, begging him to forgive her and take her away from this dreadful place. Everything had occurred so quickly that Victor, and even Harriet, were nonplussed. Finally, Victor asked, "And who is the perpetrator of this most foul abduction."

Venetia, still clinging tightly to him, pointed to Harriet, who rose in righteous indignation, prepared to defend her property. "Don't you be so high and mighty with me, sonny. That bloomin' debutante o' your'n told me she wouldn't take ya for a husband. So I took *her*. 'Course you don't much look like an old cadger to me." Harriet glared at Venetia with a belligerent expression. "Is this the one you wanted to bundle off?"

"Yes," she said but quickly added, "I didn't say he was an old cadger."

"That is quite enough!" Victor said. "My good lady, I dare not say any more than that I will relieve you of this charge, and we will be on our way directly. Good day."

"Wait a minute, you blundering idiot." Harriet stood to confront him. "You can't come in here and walk away scot-free," she shrieked. "That little vixen wormed three pounds outta me for that bloomin' gooseberry of her'n. And anyway she's promised to me mate Muldoon, and she'll fetch me a pretty penny."

Muldoon, having seen and heard the commotion, had shoved his way through the gaping crowd collected at the entrance to the parlour, and now slammed shut the door. He stood with his barking irons in his waistband and faced Victor.

"That piece o' baggage is mine, me lad," he said grimly. "And who are you to tell me different?"

Venetia trembled as she stood behind Victor, for they both noted Henry Muldoon's hand hovering menacingly over his pistols.

Old Harriet, ever the negotiator, wanted neither bloodshed nor notoriety which would adversely affect her trade and so she quickly intervened. "That one ain't worth it, Henry. All's I want, since there's a hitch, is me blunt."

But Henry was not convinced. "The bloody buck ought to be taught a lesson. Who does he think he is?"

"I beg pardon for failing to introduce myself. Most improper." Victor, who had calmly listened to the exchange between them, now handed his calling card to Muldoon. "I am Victor Auguste Alain, Marquis de Beauchante."

Someone gasped, then absolute silence fell upon the whole assemblage. The three bits o' muslin curtsied. Abbess Harriet Davenport reluctantly bowed her head while Henry Muldoon backed off and bowed in the obsequious servitude all innkeepers reserved for nobility.

"And you, I take it," said Victor, "are the proprietor of this establishment?"

"Yes indeed, your lordship. Henry Muldoon at your service. I was unaware that there was a problem. If there is anything your lordship desires—"

"I desire to depart from this place, and if you would kindly remove your flea-bitten carcass from in front of the door—"

"I do beg pardon, my lord," said Harriet, moving quickly forward. "But I have laid out good brass on this lass . . . in expectation of a goodly return, you understand."

"Good Lord!" Allen exclaimed and tossed her a pony.

"This'll do nicely, my lord. Very nicely," said Harriet as she pushed and shoved a pathway through the throng ushering Victor and Venetia to the yard, where they took their leave.

CHAPTER TEN

SHE WAS SAFE. Victor had swung Venetia up onto his horse, which he mounted behind her, and now Venetia leaned all her weight against his strong muscular chest. Never had she felt so protected as she did at this moment within his warm embrace. He had come for her. He must have known, or suspected what she... Oh, he must think her the veriest fool! But how could she have guessed, even in her wildest imaginings, that such people really existed outside novels! But Victor had known. And he had cared enough to come after her, to, dare she say, rescue her?

She was only dimly aware of the noises of travel as Victor directed his horse, retracing the route that had brought her so near doom. All that seemed real to her was the movement of the horse beneath her and the warm protection of Victor's arms. Untroubled by his silence, she was lulled into a deep contentment. The noises receded when he carefully led the horse off the main road down a steep embankment, through a marshy bog and then up an incline that led to a country lane. They travelled approximately a mile and stopped before a small inn, The Tin Cup.

Jerked alert as he slid from the horse, she cried out in alarm, "Pray don't leave me!"

"Hush," he said, reaching up for her. "We shall only stop over until my coach arrives. I left my direction and they should arrive within the hour."

"Oh,' she murmured as she slid into his arms. She had not once imagined that he could have been so orderly.

"I think it best you release your hold on me," he said, pausing before the entrance. "Such an intimate display is not at all the thing."

Obediently she moved a little away from him but kept her grip on his sleeve.

They were greeted by the innkeeper, who doubled as footman and stable-boy, for which he apologized.

"Do not trouble yourself," said Victor kindly. "We should like a small meal for the moment and when my coach arrives, I should like you to stable it. We shall stay the night and I would like two rooms, one for my sister and her maid, and one for myself. Are you able to accommodate my coachmen and horses above the stables?"

"Yes, sir, that we can," the man answered. "I'll make up your rooms directly." He first led them into the empty coffee-room, which was so quiet and peaceful that Venetia was in transports. She sank into her chair and looked at Victor.

"Mr. Allen," she said, reaching across the table to touch his hand. "I am so very grateful. I can never thank you enough."

"Well, I cannot say it was my pleasure," he grumbled, shaking his head. "You, Venetia Fielding, are a very silly, very troublesome chit!"

"Yes, so you've said." Though she had been indeed foolish, she had not lost all her dignity.

"However did you arrive at such idiotic behaviour?" he asked sternly.

"I had the best of motives, sir. Indeed, I took the path to avoid being a burden on you."

"Pray, do not do so again. I'm quite worn down by the attempt." He emitted an ironic chuckle as the landlord entered with a tray loaded with loaves of bread and rounds of cheese and a large dish of lamb cutlets, which he set on the table and then bowed to each of them and took his leave. Victor served Venetia and, without another word, began to apply himself to his own meal. Venetia watched as he ate hungrily and knew a twinge of guilt. He must be so very hungry and tired after coming such a long way for her.

"How did you know where to find me?" she asked suddenly.

"I stopped at the first town I passed and the groom at the livery had it that I might locate you at that inn." There was a wry twist to his mouth as he broke off a piece of bread. "Seems common knowledge that old Harriet's entourage never fails to stop there."

Venetia shuddered.

"Indeed." His dark eyes seemed to study her. "You are very far away from the ton. The world is not quite so prettified out here."

"I know," she whispered.

He took a swallow of ale and set his tankard on the table. "Understand one thing, Venetia. Our marriage is as painful for me as it is for you. But I must insist upon it. For you will be able to maintain your birth-right and command respect and I shall be able to retain my reputation as a gentleman.'' He leaned forward, a forbidding frown on his face. ''You must promise me that you will not attempt any further foolish notions of escape or I shall be forced to lock you in your room!''

Venetia felt a lump lodge in her throat and her eyes filled with unshed tears—tears of relief, joy and... pride. This man who was forbidding her to escape had just faced the peril of pistols to save her from unspeakable ruin. Would she try to flee from him?

''Never!'' she said.

''What?'' Victor shot up in alarm.

''You misunderstand me, sir,'' countered Venetia softly. ''What I mean is that I will never try to escape from you again.''

''Very well then.'' He smiled at her. ''Since we are soon to be wed, do you not think you might address me as Victor?''

''Yes, I should like that, Victor.'' She returned his smile and, suddenly feeling her appetite revived, daintily sampled some of the fare.

The chaise arrived in due time and Venetia was ecstatic to be reunited with her faithful Maggie. Even so, when it was time to retire, she found she was reluctant to leave Victor's side.

''Do not be such a goosecap,'' he told her. ''No one's about to kidnap you. Maggie will be with you and I'll be in the room next to yours.''

Armed with his assurance Venetia bade him goodnight and ascended to her chamber. Not until Maggie was in the trundle bed and her door securely bolted did Venetia finally crawl into her own bed.

Still she was wakeful, her mind clinging to the thought of Victor as if to a talisman. Victor, with his dark, soulful eyes, his expressive face and mercurial moods. How kind he was and how brave. She had been far more afraid than he at the sight of those menacing pistols. Her eyes fluttered open as the image of Victor handing his card to Muldoon fought to the surface of her mind. She tried to recall his words as he had introduced himself. Victor Augustus Alain. She was only vaguely aware that he had mentioned a title. A marquis?

Not that it signified. Victor was Victor, and with that she fell asleep with a smile on her lips.

THIS WAS NOT a true wedding at all, Venetia thought two days later when, having just arrived in Gretna Green, she stood in a little cottage answering the requisite questions put to her by a smithy with the stains of his trade on his hands. She confirmed that she was indeed Venetia Fielding and was present of her own free will. Victor answered the same questions in like manner and the simple ceremony was performed in the presence of Maggie and two hired witnesses. There was no music, no bridesmaid, no friends to wish them well. Venetia could not help but feel dismayed, but when Victor took her hand in a warm grip and led her back to their carriage she forced herself to smile brightly.

"We shall return to Carlisle to put up for the night," he said. "There is a much more reputable inn there and we will have better quarters this time."

It was still early evening when they reached Carlisle and pulled up at The Wild Goose, a rather spacious but relatively quiet inn. When Victor advised her he had bespoken a private parlour and suggested they dress for dinner, Venetia did not demur. In her bedchamber she refreshed herself and allowed Maggie to assist her into the gown which she had worn on the night of her betrothal party. Odd that Maggie should have brought it along, Venetia thought as she slipped into the shimmering white gown shot through with delicate gold thread.

"I thought as how you'd be likin' some pretty thing to wear for your wedding night," Maggie said.

"Thank you, Maggie" was all Venetia said. She fingered the fabric of the gown as her mind wandered back to the betrothal that had so broken her heart and was vaguely surprised that it all seemed such a very long time ago. She allowed Maggie to carefully dress her hair but she felt oddly deflated as she descended the stairs to dine with Victor.

A footman opened the door to admit her to the private dining parlour, where she found Victor alone. He advanced to greet her, and Venetia gave an involuntary gasp. She had never before realized how very handsome he was, particularly in his impeccably elegant evening attire. She looked up to meet his frankly admiring gaze and was glad that she had taken such pains with her appearance.

"You look charmingly, my dear," he said as he bent over her hand.

"And you, Victor, look the veriest Corinthian." Venetia, her spirits lifting, smiled coyly as she made him an exaggerated curtsy. "How fortunate there is such scarcity of company or I fear the ladies would snatch you from me."

"And I fear I have married a vixen with a wicked tongue!" he teased as he led her to a table set with fine china and a silver plate with a beautiful centrepiece of spring flowers between two brass candlesticks.

"Oh, how lovely," she said, turning to him with a radiant smile. *And how thoughtful.*

"I know that it wasn't the Society wedding of your dreams, Venetia," he said. "But it was true and every bit as binding. Shall we make the best of it?"

Unable to speak, she simply nodded and he pressed her hand before seating her. All at once she felt a little shy and was relieved to see a waiter appear. He brought in several steaming dishes which he set on the sideboard beside their table. They were silent as he filled their glasses from a bottle of champagne, which had been cooling in a bucket of ice.

"If you should need me, sir," he said to Victor, nodding towards the bellpull. He then exited and left them alone.

"I see we are to be accorded the privacy due a newly wed couple," Victor said, smiling as he lifted his glass in a toast. "To us."

Venetia touched her glass to his, then sipped the bubbly wine. The bubbles tickled her nose and she felt a little giddy at her boldness. This was the first time she had ever dined alone with a gentleman other than her father, but she did not feel at all awkward. Perhaps it was the champagne, though she suspected not. Her feeling of comfort was all due to Victor who put her so much at her ease with his air of composure, deferential manner and chit-chat over dinner. He encouraged her to speak about herself so that they might become better acquainted. As Venetia was at first reluctant, he quizzed her on her likes and dislikes and teased her by admitting he was surprised she had avoided trouble until she had met him.

"But I didn't," she replied with a giggle. "Stay out of trouble, that is." Without artifice she found herself launching into assorted tales of the misdeeds of her youth. She began with the time she had broken her leg by falling out of a tree she had been forbidden to climb. And the time she had been charged to mind her little brother, Cyrus, who had promptly wandered off and become lost. She credited the rescue to her mare, Cindy, who was very smart as well as being Venetia's closest companion when in summertime she and her family had rusticated at Farsdale, their country house. She even told him about the time at the academy when she had been found out for keeping a gothick novel tucked under her pillow. She had almost been expelled, but when the headmistress took the book away from her, she had disappeared for days and never said another word on the subject!

Victor laughed heartily as she recounted her numerous scrapes, and Venetia found she enjoyed making him laugh. It wasn't until after the sweetmeats and coffee were served that she recalled that her mama had often counselled her to encourage a gentleman to speak about himself to best entertain him. But Venetia did not feel the need to entertain Victor, for they were not lacking in enjoyment. Yet she did long to know so much more about him and was just about to enquire when he spoke.

"I have something that belongs to you," he said, holding out her pearl necklace.

"Oh, you never sold it! I thought . . ." She stopped as suspicion dawned. "You never intended to sell the necklace, did you?"

Victor's mouth curved into a wry grin. "I confess my sins, but I was sorely tempted. I admit I was rather uncertain about its fate were I to leave it in the hands of such a harum-scarum as yourself. Conversely, I was rather reluctant to part with such a valuable item for a mere fraction of its worth."

"I hardly thought you capable of such deception, Victor!" she said, bristling. But when she looked across at him, he was smiling gently. The look in his eyes revealed more eloquently than words that he had not sold the necklace because he had not wished her to leave his protection.

"How could I have been so mistaken in your character? You are the kindest man I have ever known," Venetia said in a watery voice.

"Here now, my dear. You ain't going to turn into a watering pot on me, are you? Gowned as you are, I think these will suit very well," he said, and stood up to fasten the pearls round her neck. The touch of his fingers on her naked skin produced a pleasant sensation of radiating warmth. She swallowed, hoping she was not blushing.

"Thank you," she managed to say.

"And," he said, taking a small jeweller's box from his breast pocket, "I thought these might complete the set. Would the bride, reluctant though she may be, please accept this small token of esteem from the groom in hopes that we may contrive to rub along tolerably well?"

"Oh, Victor," she whispered, quite overcome as she opened the little box to reveal earrings that perfectly matched her pearls. "They're beautiful. But you needn't have gone to such expense. And not for a wife you had thrust upon you."

"Mere frippery, I assure you. Picked them up at Rundell's, thinking they might cheer you," he said almost apologetically.

"I don't know what to say," she said with a catch in her voice. Though he had always known her plans to leave him by any means, he had only thought of her happiness.

"You mustn't cry, my dear," he said. "Pearls are no reason for tears. And presents ought to make you smile, not cry."

"But I don't deserve them. I've been so much trouble to you," she blubbered.

"Come now, buck up, there's a good girl. You've had a long day, my wife, and you are fatigued. The wedding feast is over and now off to bed with you," he said, stroking one of her curls and turning her towards the door.

She made her way to her room, glad to escape before she made a complete cake of herself. Victor Allen had proved yet again to be the kindest man of her acquaintance. He had gone to great lengths to do all he could to make this marriage that neither wanted as palatable as possible, while she had been an ungrateful wretch. She looked down at the simple wedding band. It was real gold. The marriage was just as real, as Victor had said, and binding. At that moment, she decided she would be a good wife and a real wife.

Thusly, she prepared for her wedding night. Maggie assisted her into the sheer negligee set that she had selected so carefully for the duke. Completely white, and made of aerophane crepe, both negligee and slip were trimmed with a light smattering of lace and seed pearls. It was very beautiful, very sheer and as delicate as she herself felt.

She allowed Maggie to brush out her long curls and then dismissed her.

Venetia looked at herself in the tiny mirror set on the dressing table. Her hair fell bright and glowing about her shoulders. Would Victor find her beautiful? She tentatively slipped off the negligee and found she felt very exposed wearing only the sheer under gown. She reached for the negligee again, but stopped herself mid-motion. She would not be missish, for Victor was a kind decent gentleman. And she meant to fulfil her vow that she would be a good wife.

She slipped into bed, eyes wide with anticipation and apprehension. She waited, and waited, but Victor did not come to her.

At last, Venetia gave up hope, and unable to decide whether she was gravely disappointed or vastly relieved, she fell asleep.

CHAPTER ELEVEN

THEY ARRIVED back at 41 Fitzroy Square in the midst of a steady drizzle and a decided chill in the air. Venetia's eyes automaticaly sought out the sign Victor Allen, Portraits. While it did seem brighter, having been washed cleaner by the rain, it was still hung askew. She would fix that instantly.

"Venetia?" Victor, she saw, was waiting to hand her down from the carriage.

"Thank you," she said, reaching out her hand. But to her surprise he didn't take it. Instead he lifted her in his arms and carried her safely over the puddles now forming in the square, up the steps and through the door that had been opened by a smiling Jonathan.

"Welcome home, Mr. and Mrs. Allen," said the manservant cheerfully, then excused himself to assist with the unloading of the luggage.

Neither of them had responded to his greeting. Venetia, still a little shocked at finding herself nestled in Victor's arms, was struggling to deny the warm sweet sensation that was gripping her. And why was Victor staring at her as if he had never seen her before? His arms had tightened about her, his dark eyes were kindling in a strange way and his mouth was hovering so tantalizingly close to hers. Her pulse raced and she held her breath as intuitively her lips parted.

Abruptly he set her down.

"Dashed bad weather," he said as he shed his coat. Venetia, straining to compose herself, watched him shake the water from his hat and toss both garments over the nearby bannister. "Hope Jonathan has fires laid."

Venetia hoped so as well. She looked at the puddles forming on the tiled floor of the hall entrance and wondered if it was the rain that made the house seem even more dismal than it had the first day she entered it. Or was it the ennui that had suddenly descended upon her?

"Come," Victor said pleasantly. "I'll show you to your room."

Venetia looked questioningly at him.

"I instructed Jonathan to prepare the room next to mine for you," he explained, his expression quite ordinary. "I thought that under the circumstances, it would present a better appearance. And Maggie shall have one of the rooms belowstairs. You do want to keep her with you, don't you?"

"That would please me very much, Victor," Venetia replied with equanimity.

Upstairs he led her to the end of the hall and opened a door upon a sitting-room which contained a small bookcase filled with rows of reading material, a sofa, a small table and two very comfortable-looking chairs. Though the whole presented a cosy aspect, the room significantly lacked for something. A door on the right opened on a large bedchamber complete with dressing-room.

"Those will be your rooms," Victor said as Venetia looked at the plain furnishings and bare walls and pulled her cloak closer about her. The fireplace had been laid but was not lit.

Victor bent to kindle the fire. "There. A cheerful fire will soon make you comfortable," he said as the logs caught and flared. He stood regarding her. "You will still have privacy even though my bedchamber opens upon the sitting-room which we will share. You won't mind that, I hope?"

"No. Of course not," Venetia said. So they were to each live privately. And only a few minutes ago she had so eagerly responded in his arms and had foolishly hoped... She had underestimated him once again. Victor was a gentleman who, knowing she had no choice but to agree to a marriage of convenience, would not force his attentions upon her. Yet he would be sure that she received all the respect and deference due as his wife. She smiled at him. "Thank you. I shall be quite comfortable here."

She would see that Victor received the same respect and deference due to him, she thought as he left her. The very instruction she would issue the next morning as Mrs. Victor Allen would be for Jonathan to straighten and polish the sign.

DAMN! He had married a child, and much against her will, Victor thought as he bent to light the fire in his own bedchamber. Best he not forget it.

Only... even though she was as light as a feather in his arms, she had felt very much like a woman. And the way she had stared at him with those wide green eyes, her sweetly curved lips parted and... willing? Gad! He must be all about in his head to think of bedding her as easily as one did a common wench... or a wife?

He stood up and kicked at a log that came loose. His wife? Child or woman, she was a lady. A lady bred and born to become the wife of a peer. And she was saddled with him. And, damn it, he was saddled with her. He ran a hand distractedly through his hair and strode about the room. Was there ever such a coil!

After a few moments, he stopped before the window, his hands clasped tightly behind his back. At any rate, they had scotched a scandal. Oh, there might still be some idle gossip for a bit, until a more juicy on-dit took precedence. Then their marriage would be a nine-day wonder and Venetia would still be an extraordinarily beautiful woman, enticing enough to attract any man. If only there were some way he could think of to gracefully undo the marriage.

Divorce would only portend another scandal. But annulment was a distinct possibility. He watched the rain, heavier now as it pelted against the window pane, while he pondered this new idea. The law would only require proof that after three years the marriage had not been consummated.

Victor considered this carefully. He doubted that Venetia would much mind his absence from her bed, but for himself it could prove more difficult. Yet, he would be more than willing should there come along a man more worthy of her. Even such a one as Bertram.

Mon Dieu! Bertram was certain to tire of his mistress in three years' time. There was his answer.

IN THE DAYS that followed, Venetia found that she received very little more attention from Victor as his wife than she had received as an unwanted houseguest. They shared the sitting-room which connected their bedchambers, but he seldom visited it. However, since she was no longer confined to her rooms she did encounter him at meals and at the evening gathering in the parlour from which she was no longer excluded. She was grateful, for she was eager to listen to Charles's latest episodes of the street urchins' adventures. She was also eager to encourage Linda in her quest for a solo singing career, though Venetia knew Linda had neither the talent nor temperament.

Venetia was not possessed of an idle nature and soon her days also became filled. Though theirs was only a marriage of convenience, she was too conscientious to neglect any of the duties incumbent upon her in her newly acquired status. In her household, menus would be planned and delicious meals properly served. Venetia employed Maggie as her emissary and was pleased to learn that Bella readily agreed to follow the menus and was merry as a grig to send Maggie to do her marketing, which was a vast relief to Annie, the hapless scullery maid.

In another matter Venetia felt herself at point non plus. Victor's house was vast and noted for its hospitality. And no one, including Victor, seemed to have a care that it was also dingy, unkempt and as unattractive as an old barn. At each turn, Venetia was confronted by more evidence of decay, and now being resigned that this was indeed the house in which she would dwell a lifetime, felt it only proper that she do what was necessary to make the house comfortable to live in for herself, as well. But, remembering how Victor had responded with rage when she had tidied his studio, she was hesitant to approach him. Instead, she applied to Jonathan.

"Is there someone employed to do housecleaning duties?" she asked.

Jonathan, who was clearing away the breakfast dishes, paused and grinned at her. "I fear madam, it is, so to speak, rather a slipshod arrangement. Annie does what she can when Bella can spare her from the scullery, and oftentimes Josie lends a hand when she is, er, in residence.

Venetia brightened. Two maids would certainly be sufficient, and with Maggie to supervise . . .

"Is Josie in residence now?"

"No, madam. At present she is residing with a, er, friend. But, for a few shillings, she might be persuaded to return."

"Excellent, Jonathan. Then will you . . . ?" Venetia hesitated. Where was she to come by the shillings?

Jonathan kept his eyes lowered as he cleaned the table.

"Certainly, madam. And I will arrange for the shillings."

"Thank you, Jonathan. If you would be so kind."
Again she hesitated, looking anxiously at him. "You
don't imagine Vic…Mr. Allen would object, do you?"

The corner of the servant's mouth twitched. "I
think you will find, madam, that Monsieur Allen is
only vaguely aware of anything that does not affect his
garret or his painting."

Jonathan was as good as his word, and only a few
days later, Josie returned to residence.

Josie proved to be an excellent and hard worker.
Annie, however, even under Maggie's supervision, was
as lackadaisical about housecleaning as she had been
about the marketing. And since the house was so vast,
the task so monumental, Venetia, anxious to accom-
plish as much as possible as soon as possible, decided
she could also lend a hand. Jonathan, too, proved to
be a valuable ally. In spite of the innumerable duties
he performed for Victor, he did not hesitate to pitch in
whenever he was able. Each time Venetia required
money for additions or repairs, Jonathan would
magically produce the necessary funds. Venetia did
not need to enquire as to the source of Jonathan's
pounds and pence, for she knew full well that they
came from the bowl in Victor's garret.

JONATHAN WAS QUITE RIGHT about Victor's being
oblivious to what did not immediately concern his
work. But only a blind man could have been unaware
that the house was taking on a cleaner, brighter aspect, and when Victor encountered a workman employed at plastering in the entrance hall, he observed
to no one in particular that such repairs were long

overdue. Otherwise he took no heed of what was transpiring.

However, Victor was an aesthete who not only created but was highly sensitive to art and beauty, whether he observed it in nature, in humans or a particular part of the human anatomy. So it was that upon racing up his porch steps and entering his own house one day, he was stopped short by the sight of a dainty well-turned ankle supported by a small slender unshod foot poised on tiptoe on the seat of a chair.

Stifling his fascination at such a staggering sight, Victor forced his gaze to travel upward. As he did so, he first encountered the full skirt of a bright blue muslin dress splashed with red roses and hitched in an unseemly fashion to a tiny waist suggestive of a shapely figure. As he gazed further up, he was welcomed to the sight of a small but well-rounded bosom swelling beneath an apron of fustian. The graceful neck was topped by a luscious riot of red curls held back by a bright yellow scarf. The profile was a picture of perfection. The dainty nose, the wide green eyes... Venetia!

"What the devil are you playing at?" he shouted.

Venetia started, almost dropping but managing to safely balance the picture she was about to hang before turning to look down at him.

"I thought this picture would look well here," she explained. "It's one of many you had stored away and I thought you wouldn't mind. Do you?" Her voice faded and her eyes widened and she looked down at him with some trepidation.

Victor paid not the slightest heed to what she was saying. His eyes studied her intently, his intuitive artistic perception already engaged. "Do not move. Stay just as you are," he ordered. He circled the chair on which she stood, studying her from every angle.

Her anxious expression changed to one of incredulity. "What...what are you doing, Mr. Allen? Is there something wrong?"

"*Non, ma petite.* Just the opposite. *Parfait,*" he said, and added several admiring phrases in French. "Come." He reached up to help her down. "I wish you to come with me."

"With you? Where?" Venetia asked as she bent to put on her slippers.

"We shall take a ride to just outside of Town. I want to paint."

She nodded. She knew that Victor did nature scenes which he sold to a local merchant to supplement his portrait work. Hadn't she been hanging the ones he had discarded as worthless (and she thought priceless) all over the house? Thank goodness Jonathan had stored them away. But why would she need to accompany him?

"Wait here, if you please. I'll just bundle up a few things," he said, and started towards the stairs.

"And I'll change while you're doing that," Venetia said, following him.

He turned so abruptly that she was forced to step back. "You will not change a thing! I want you just as you are. And we must hurry. I must get there before sunset."

Venetia watched him in puzzlement and some agitation as he bounded up the stairs. How could he wish her to appear in the streets in this old skirt, no stockings and dirty apron? She would be mortified. But he had been so emphatic, she was afraid to disobey. Still...

"Hadn't I better remove this?" she said tentatively, starting to untie the apron when he returned with brushes and sketching book.

"Absolutely not," he said. "Come along."

Jonathan, who had followed his master carrying a box filled with small paint pots, understood. "I'll have Maggie fetch a cloak for you, madam," he said.

But when Venetia emerged from the house she forgot all about what she was wearing. Her eyes focussed on the pretty little black mare harnessed to a shiny black tilbury.

"Oh, she's a beauty!" she exclaimed, and walked over to rub the neck of the sleek little mare who was being held by Oliver, the errand boy whom she had first seen in Victor's studio. He grinned at her.

"She's called Tiny 'cause that's wot she be. But that don't mean she ain't a real sweet goer, mum."

"Is she yours?" she asked Victor when she was seated beside him and he was expertly manoeuvring the tilbury out of the square.

He nodded and she was silent until he had directed the carriage through the city traffic onto the turnpike, where he quickened the pace.

"Oh, this is famous!" Venetia exclaimed. "She is a real sweet goer! Just like my Cindy."

He sent her a quick glance. "You miss her?"

Her nod was slow and pensive. Never again would she gallop freely over the Farsdale meadows on the little mare who had been her pride and joy.

"Would you like to take the reins?" he asked.

"Oh, could I?" she cried. He smiled and handed over the ribbons. Venetia almost laughed aloud as she set the little mare sprinting down the almost deserted highway at a fast gallop. The day was bright and sunny, and the warm breeze that whistled through her hair made her feel almost free. It had been such a long time. . . .

"You're an excellent whipster," said Victor. Venetia, engrossed, only nodded her thanks. But when he added that the mare and gig were available to her at any time, she turned a grateful face to him. "Just send a note to Turner," he added. "They are stabled at his livery."

A short time later, Victor took the reins back and turned off into a small lane thickly bordered by hedgerows on either side. The sun was obscured by the dense foliage, and Venetia felt as if they were travelling deeper and deeper into a forest.

"Where are we going?" she asked.

"To visit the gypsies."

"Gypsies!" she exclaimed, turning to him in quick alarm. She had never actually seen a gypsy but she knew they were people to avoid at any cost. She shuddered as she remembered the long-ago threats of her nanny, "Don't you stray from me, child. The gypsies will surely get you!"

"Do not fear," said Victor, gently touching her cheek. "They won't steal my gypsy girl from me. They are my friends."

She stared at him. *Gypsy girl?*

He chuckled. "You could be one of them, you know, in your present costume. Most of them are dark but some have red hair and many have green eyes—not like yours, of course. But I think you will pass."

"Pass?" she asked, puzzled.

He nodded. "With you in that peasant garb, the gypsies will accept you as one of them. And then, with the camp setting and ... other things, I will paint the most remarkable picture."

"Oh, Victor," she giggled. "Can you really picture me as a gypsy?"

"*Mais oui!* With your glorious hair, overwhelming beauty and certain, er, particularly enticing features," he said, "you look just the part." The suggestive smile hovering about his lips caused her to blush.

They rounded a curve and came out of the forest upon a clearing and a spectacular scene. Venetia held her breath, trying to absorb all the impressions at once. She first saw the gaudily painted house wagons formed in a circle with the livestock tethered nearby. There were many horses, several cows and too many goats to count. And the gypsies, numbering over a hundred, Venetia thought, if one were to count the children. There were children everywhere—rolling on the grass, chasing the dogs or diving in and out of the stream where women washed their clothing. The women all wore full bright skirts and vast amounts of jewellery and all were busy, some washing clothes, others cooking, and some filling buckets of water from a clear spring that bubbled through a mountain crevice. Still others were carrying wood to feed the fire in the centre of the campsite. The men wore bright blousy shirts with loose sleeves and tight pants held at the waist by brightly coloured scarves. They lolled about the fire or leaned against the wagons, talking, smoking and drinking from bottles of wine. They were powerfully built men with swarthy skin, but they didn't look at all ferocious. In fact the scene was oddly domestic. Still, Venetia instinctively reached for Victor's hand. But he had already alighted and come round to hand her down.

"I promise you have nothing to fear," he said, grinning.

"Veector! Welcome, old friend," came a hearty shout, and Venetia turned to see one of the men approaching them. He wore a red bandana around his dark hair and a big loop earring that dangled from one ear. She stared at him and he stared back. Though rather disconcerted, Venetia noted that his eyes were indeed a greenish colour. "And you have brought us a very beautiful visitor, as well," he said, bowing before her. "Welcome, my lady."

Victor, who was unloading his painting gear, glanced at him. "Hello, Sergei. Good to see you again." He turned to stand beside Venetia. "This is Sergei," he told her. "The patriarch or head of this caravan. Sergei, may I present my wife, Venetia."

"Ah, my lady, this is indeed a pleasure." Again he bowed to her. "Veector, you sly fox! You never even hinted. Come see what good fortune has befallen our friend," he called, and two other men joined them and were introduced. Both bowed before Venetia, gazed admiringly at her and teased Victor good-naturedly.

"Anna, come!" Sergei called, and a pleasingly plump woman with rather deep mysterious eyes emerged from one of the wagons. She too had red hair but liberally streaked with gray.

"Veector!" she boomed, "How are you?" Then she noticed Venetia. "Welcome, my dear. And who is this?"

Sergei answered. "This is Veector's woman. His wife. And you must tell her her fortune."

"You must indeed," said Victor. "The true one. Not what she wants to hear," he added with a knowing smile as he opened his arms to embrace the woman.

Venetia smiled her agreement and greeted Anna as well as others of the elders who had come forward to acknowledge their presence. They all knew and seemed to love Victor and referred to him by his French title. Venetia was able to discern that much as they bantered back and forth in English and another language she was not acquainted with.

Someone helped Victor unload his equipment and another woman took charge of his horse and carriage.

Victor advised the gathering that he wished to complete his sketching while the sun was still high, and asked Anna to loan Venetia some jewellery and a chain bracelet for her ankle. "Take off your slippers, my dear," he said to Venetia, who glanced round to see that most of the gypsy women were barefoot. "I want to paint you amongst my friends. Just move about the camp with Anna and enjoy yourself.''

To her surprise Venetia did just that. She felt quite glamorous in the jewellery Anna had abundantly decorated her with—the several necklaces of coins around her neck, large gold hoops for her ears, bangles on her arms and a chain around her ankle. The touch of the grass and warm earth against her bare feet gave her a wild uninhibited feeling as she moved about the campsite with Anna, entering into the many activities with ease. She played with the children and talked with the women, completely fascinated with a style of life so different from her own. She enjoyed herself immensely and was almost completely oblivious of Victor, who followed her from one setting to another, rapidly sketching.

''Come,'' said Anna as the sun began to lower. ''It will soon be time for the feast and I promised to tell your fortune.'' She glanced towards Victor, who nodded, and then led Venetia to the largest and most colourful wagon in the caravan.

Venetia, climbing into the strange house, was surprised to find it so roomy, so cool and comfortable.

''When and where were you and Veector married?'' asked Anna, motioning her to a seat in front of a small table.

''A month ago at Gretna Green.'' Venetia fervently hoped her whisker would not be found out, for they had really been married less than a fortnight.

Anna's eyes danced. ''So! Then you must know your husband well. Does he satisfy you?'' she asked.

Venetia's jaw dropped, her eyes widened and the blood rushed to her face. Anna's laugh was so knowing that Venetia could not mistake her meaning. She opened her mouth to answer but only emitted a barely audible gasp.

Anna, who immediately understood her dismay, said, "Your time will come." She gave a dismissive wave of her hand as if to say she need not answer.

The gesture left Venetia relieved but feeling a little stunned, as if she had been smitten with a club. She managed a weak smile and said, "Mr. Al... Victor is a very kind and gentle man."

"Indeed he is," said Anna as she spread a cloth upon the little table in anticipation of the fortune-telling. "He is a brave and honest man, too. My Sergei would be holed in Newgate were it not for Veector Alain!"

"Oh?" said Venetia, much interested.

"Yes, indeed. They were going to clap him in irons just for pinching an old goblet worth only two pounds and four shillings. Had it not been for Veector's kindness to refund the money and defend Sergei's character, he would not be a free man today...." She shook her head. "'Tis no sin, you know, to take sixpence or a shilling or two from them that has it to spare."

Venetia tried to comprehend this unusual philosophy as she watched Anna set a deck of cards upon the table.

"Now, little one, I shall tell your fortune, the real one." The gypsy woman smiled as she reached for Venetia's hand and peered intently at her palm, then closed her eyes and sought guidance from the great beyond to reveal what lay in store for Venetia Fielding Alain. Venetia's heart pounded and she watched in fearful anticipation as the seemingly strange woman began to lay out the cards face up. There was a pause during which Anna seemed to be gathering information. Then she spoke in a low voice of Venetia's little brother, her mare and Farsdale in such detail that Venetia was shocked into belief. Then this was indeed to be her real fortune.

The spell was broken when Anna abruptly broke off. "All that is gone. Over and done with. We must look at what lies before you, the path you will follow as the wise men followed the star." She was silent for a time, slowly laying out each card, but when the queen of hearts appeared she smiled. "Ah! One child you will have. As beautiful as yourself with the same bright red hair."

Venetia felt a happy longing stir within her. But how could she have a child when she didn't really have a husband? Could this truly be her real fortune? Hampered by doubts, she looked at Anna, who was intent upon the cards. Suddenly she gave a gasp that made Venetia jump.

"Don't, I pray you, let it escape!" Anna said, the deep mysterious eyes fastening upon Venetia's. "Reach for it and guard it with your life!" she said as a long finger tapped the ten of diamonds.

"Whaat . . . what is it?" Venetia asked.

"The most priceless treasure on earth to the one lucky enough to have found it," Anna answered emphatically. "But you must grasp it and hold fast!"

"But when...how?" Venetia gazed at her in as much terror as anticipation. How could she, if she didn't know what or where it was?

"In good time, my dear. You will know," Anna said as she began to turn over other cards. "An enemy!" she croaked as the queen of spades appeared. "She would take your treasure from you, this woman with flaxen hair. You must not let her." Anna stopped and began to gather the cards.

Venetia, rapt with attention, asked, "Who is she? What more can you tell me?"

"There is nothing to fear. Just beware," said Anna. "And that is all for now. It's time for the feast."

Venetia, still full of questions, had no choice but to follow Anna to the centre of the campsite, where everyone had gathered around the fire and the women were already serving the food. Anna, giving her two wooden bowls and spoons, instructed her to serve her husband first. It was the custom.

Venetia filled a bowl from the communal pot as she had seen the other women do and carried it to Victor.

"Thank you," he said, a smug smile on his face. "I'm happy to see that you are learning your station."

"And I am happy to see that you are enjoying it," she said, as, joining in his teasing mood, she deliberately leaned down, lowering her bosom closer to him than necessary. "For I assure you, the lesson will not last long."

Victor felt his heart leap at the provocative gesture. His gaze followed her as she turned back to fill her own bowl. Her slender figure swayed gracefully, her bare feet lightly touching the ground, a gold chain around an enticing ankle barely visible under her full skirt. She had been good-natured, he thought, accompanying him without complaint, and entering wholeheartedly into the adventure. Except for her unusually fair skin she might have truly been one of the gypsy women and he had made several excellent sketches. From these would emerge many paintings of great beauty and worthy social comment. Venetia returned to sit beside him, and he watched with tender amusement as she stared at the contents of her bowl.

"It will not bite you," he whispered. "Just taste it."

She glanced suspiciously at him but tentatively sampled the gruel. She smiled, nodded and began to eat. But when she took a small sip of the ale he saw her eyes water as she swallowed convulsively several times and glanced self-consciously around. No one seemed to have noticed. A bit later he unobstrusively exchanged his empty mug for her full one. Her grateful smile warmed him, and he felt a strange contentment in this close camaraderie they shared. And a strange remorse when Anna pulled her away.

"Come," said the gypsy queen. "The women dance." And in a moment Venetia was twirling with the gypsy women before the men to the lively tunes of the mandolins. Victor again took up his charcoal and sketch-book but he couldn't take his eyes from Venetia. Her red hair, loosed from its scarf, fell to her waist and swung about her shoulders as she frollicked in the dance. She was laughing and, with a natural grace and ease, she followed the steps as if she had done them all her life. The charcoal rested idly in Victor's hand as he watched in fascination. The way her full skirt billowed about and her delightful bare feet tripped in rhythm to the beat of the music made his heart pulse in unison.

"Ah, Veector, you lucky one!" said Sergei beside him. "So! You have found your true love!"

"Eh?" Victor, startled out of his reverie, turned towards him.

"But you are not truly married!" grinned Sergei.

"Eh?" Victor repeated, wondering how the devil his gypsy friend could know.

Sergei laughed heartly at his friend's discomfort.

"Not until you have performed the true ritual—gypsy fashion," he said.

"Oh, yes, quite," Victor said with great relief. "And what would that be?"

"You must steal her away to your wagon and make her one with you."

"But I have no wagon," Victor said with a sheepish grin.

"True," agreed Sergei, chuckling. "And since you have already made her one with you, a wagon is no longer necessary. But the gypsies might settle for a flight into the forest and a kiss!" He gestured towards the dancing women. "But first, you must steal her from the crowd and announce to one and all that she belongs to you alone!"

She belongs to you alone. The words stung and Victor flushed hotly. He had never been so moved. Quickly he looked again at Venetia, and began to feel his thin veneer of distance dissolve. In its place soared desire and the undeniable urge to call this beautiful woman his.

"Come, my friend, don't be shy!" urged Sergei.

Boisterous shouts rose from the men as Victor strode into the circle and seized Venetia and flung her over his shoulder.

"What are you doing?" she screeched in a voice which Victor fervently prayed no one could hear. "Mr. Allen, what's come over you? Put me down!"

"Be still!" he whispered frantically as he broke through the circle of laughing men. "And do me the honour of at least looking pleased."

"But what are you doing?" she asked, and more urgently as he dashed amongst the trees, "Where are you taking me?"

"Calm yourself, Venetia. It's only a gypsy ritual," he assured her. Seeing that they had arrived about ten feet into the forest, he gently slid her from his shoulder.

"A ritual? But what sort? Ouch!" she screamed, flinging her arms tight about his neck. "Something bit me, Victor!"

"Shh...let me look," he said, sitting on a tree trunk and pulling her onto his lap.

"It's my foot! And it won't let it go!" she cried, burying her face against his chest.

He lifted her foot, from which a twig dangled from a thorn that had pierced her soft flesh. He gently extracted it. "Just a thorn," he soothed. "It will be all right. I know it hurts but this will ease the pain," he said as he bent to kiss the wound. "At least my mother always said it would," he added, smiling at her.

Venetia's breath caught as she relaxed her hold on him. She gave a nervous chuckle. "How silly of me. I imagined it could only have been a snake and...I'm deathly afraid of snakes." She looked up at him, her lips parted in that warm inviting way he had seen once before, and Victor could not help himself. He did what he had been wanting to do all day long. He kissed her.

It was like taking a long draught of warm, wild, intoxicating wine. His senses reeled and he throbbed with a passion unlike any he had felt before. A passion tender and gentle, yet so urgent that he was filled with a desire to lift her in his arms and run to where they could truly be alone and he could make her one with him.

CHAPTER TWELVE

THE GYPSIES' goodbyes were as overwhelming as their welcome had been. Sergei and Anna, along with other members of the elders, accompanied them to their carriage, offering incantations for their good health and fortune, and inviting them both to return when the caravan again made the yearly trek to this area. Anna embraced Venetia and Victor before sending them on their way.

As the carriage wound through the hedgerows to the highway, Venetia looked at the bangles on her arms, which, along with the dainty chain still around her ankle and the fob chain for Victor, were all they had allowed the generous Anna to press upon them. The pieces looked to be real gold and Venetia wondered if they were. She also wondered if they were stolen.

'Tis no sin to take from them that has . . . But having been raised to believe stealing *was* a sin, she was confused. Venetia looked across at Victor and would have asked him for his opinion, but his eyes were intent upon the road, his expression withdrawn and forbidding. He had been that way since their flight into the forest. She swallowed, remembering the shared intimacy. She had felt secure in the warm gentle protection of his arms. Even when he had tenderly

touched his lips to her foot it had seemed natural and
sweet, and a delicious tremor of pleasure had swept
through her. But when he had kissed her... Venetia
drew in a quick breath. Never in all her life had she
been kissed with such passion—or even kissed at all.
Nothing had prepared her for the flood of feelings she
had succumbed to when Victor's mouth had claimed
hers. She had felt such a wave of yearning to belong to
him, to become completely his.

But he had suddenly pulled away and become cold,
almost as if angry. He had carried her through the
brambles back to the gypsy camp in silence.

They had greeted them with ribald laughter and ris-
qué remarks that had made Venetia blush. Victor accepted their good-natured teasing but had hardly
uttered another word to her. Gone was the intimacy,
the warm companionship they had so briefly shared.

Venetia suddenly grew angry. It seemed all too clear
that he regretted the intimacy, she thought, her lips
tightening. But that did not give him the right to spoil
what had been for her a delightful day. She had felt an
unusually happy sense of freedom amongst those
people who lived so naturally. And Victor had seemed
to enjoy her happiness. He had encouraged her and
instructed her. In fact, she had thought they had become friends. She was not about to be played for a
fool!

"Would you say this is stolen?" she asked.

"Did you speak?" Victor's head jerked as if he was
pulled from some reverie of his own, and he looked
surprised to see her sitting beside him.

"I asked if you thought this was stolen," she repeated, tapping the bangle around her wrist.

His mouth twitched. "Probably."

"Perhaps I'd best not wear it, then," she said, fearful of coming across the original owner.

Victor chuckled. "Never fear. My friends are unscrupulous but extremely clever. They never distribute their wares until well out of the vicinity in which they were, er, acquired."

She looked up at him. "Anna told me how you came to Sergei's defence when he pinched . . . stole a goblet, and it was you who kept him from going to gaol. Did you know him then?"

Victor shook his head. "Just happened to be in the shop when the incident occurred."

"You mean to say you defended a perfect stranger caught in the act of stealing?" she enquired. Then more hesitantly, she asked, "Do you believe as they do, that stealing is not a sin?"

Victor shrugged. "That is not for me to say," he replied. They were on the turnpike now, and he was silent as he manoeuvred their carriage around a wagon loaded with hay. Then he looked at her. "Besides, who am I to judge? Gypsies, you know, believe they have a God-given right to steal."

"How can they think so?" Venetia asked with more curiosity than outrage.

"Because, as legend has it, they stole the sixth nail that was meant to help fasten the body of Christ to the cross. The nail that was to have pierced his heart."

"Oh, I see," she said, reminded of Anna's reference to the wise men who followed the star.

"Everybody steals something," Victor mused. "Perhaps I stole something when I paid for the goblet."

"You could not have stolen it if you paid for it," she countered.

"I paid for the goblet, yes, but I stole Sergei's friendship, which for the past three years has afforded me the privilege to set up my canvas amongst them and paint to my heart's content. A very profitable investment for me."

No, she thought, Victor was not that shrewd in his dealings with people. He had instinctively come to the rescue of a man in trouble. For that was Victor's way. And it was not in Victor's nature to judge. He granted the gypsies the right to their own philosophy just as he had granted Harriet Davenport the right to her trade. He hadn't been angry. He had cheerfully paid her for Venetia's release and had never yet said one word against her. Venetia felt a chill as she recalled her narrow escape. She drew her feet onto the seat and covered them with her cloak.

"What's amiss?" asked Victor.

"It's becoming cool," she answered. "And I'm a bit chilled."

He frowned. "I'm can't say I'm surprised. Running about with no stockings."

She stared at him, aghast. "I beg your pardon. I seem to recall that it was you who particularly asked that I remove my shoes and—"

"Oh, yes, that," he muttered. "But more to the point is why the devil were you dressed like a common servant in the first place?"

"When one is performing the duties of a servant, my good man," snapped Venetia, her temper rising, "one is apt to look the part."

"Well, my girl, don't ring a peal over me! I certainly did not ask you to perform such chores."

"Of course not. You do not care a rap that we reside in a dusty, disorganized, cluttered house! You just hide yourself away in your dusty, disorganized, cluttered garret and calmly disarrange your paint pots so you can find them!"

To her surprise he laughed. "Touché!"

"Mr. Allen," she said firmly. "It is no laughing matter! Your cavalier attitude in regard to this serious matter is most unbecoming! The condition of your residence and studio is deplorable and unworthy of your artistry." She set her feet firmly on the floor of the chaise, her arms crossed tightly across her chest as she continued. "Furthermore, Mr. Allen, I am convinced the deplorable appearance of your house has a damaging effect on your business. What woman of Quality enjoys sitting in such a—" She broke off as he leaned across and placed a hand over her mouth.

"My name is Victor. And you have said enough. You have obviously proven your talent and ability to run a household. Then pray continue, but as a lady. Not a common servant." He removed his hand from her mouth and she gasped.

"Mr. Allen...Victor," she amended angrily. "With what am I to perform my duties?"

"Meaning?" he asked in honest innocence.

"I refer to a household budget. Money. An allowance to hire adequate help and defray the expense of a well-run household. Then, sir, I assure you I shall be happy to assume my position as lady of the house." She sank back in her seat exhausted, red-faced and somewhat relieved. She had spoken her piece and she was glad of it!

"Venetia, money is and has always been available to you. Just take whatever you need from my—"

She sat up quite straight. "Victor Allen, I am your wife! And if you think I shall resort to rummaging through your open cash-box for what I require like any beggar or gambler who pulls on you, you are greatly mistaken! I should not stoop to such debasement!"

Victor rubbed his chin with a mixture of amusement and surprise. "Forgive me, Mrs. Allen, for making such an error in etiquette." He inclined his head and his mouth twisted into an ironic smile. "I will speak to my man of business, Mr. . . . er, Latimer, and adjure him to make immediate arrangements to accommodate your needs." If gypsies could steal, he could lie, Victor told himself. It was only a slightly premature lie. Laurent had been begging after him for years to solicit the services of Latimer, Laurent's own man of business. He would engage him first thing in the morning.

WHEN A MR. LATIMER called upon her two mornings later, Venetia received him in the small withdrawing-room. He was a short, slender man of middle years fastidiously attired in a dark coat and breeches.

"Mrs. Allen," he said respectfully as he bowed over her hand. "Edward Latimer at your service."

"Thank you. I am delighted to meet you," she said politely. "You, I understand, are my husband's man of business?"

"That is correct, madam."

"And you have been in his employ for some time?" she asked dubiously, not glancing at the escritoire, which she knew to be littered with a variety of notes, unpaid accounts and often a forgotten cheque or two. She glanced again at the gentleman, and while the grey eyes seemed intelligent enough, she wondered at his efficiency if he could allow such disarray...

"Just so." Mr. Latimer's thin lips grimaced ever so slightly. "That is, er, some aspects Mr. Allen has, er, preferred to handle himself. But now, due to an increase in his clientele, along with his recent marriage, he has asked me to take complete charge of his business affairs."

"I see," said Venetia, somewhat relieved.

"I am to set up a separate account for you, madam, for whatever you require for household expenses, as well as an allowance for your personal needs. So, if we could discuss these requirements..."

"Oh, yes indeed," she said eagerly. "Do sit down, Mr. Latimer."

In the days that followed, possibly owing to Victor's preoccupation with his painting or his lack of interest in business matters, Mr. Latimer fell into the habit of applying to Venetia in regard to Victor's requirements, as well. Venetia, resolutely and diplomatically, applied to Victor.

"Do you mind if Mr. Latimer examines the papers in your desk? There seem to be some overdue accounts," or "Mr. Latimer seems to think that if you were to permit him to handle the commissions and collections on your paintings..."

To all of which Victor would nod in absent agreement, apparently happy to leave such matters to someone else, freeing him for the work he enjoyed most.

Mr. Latimer was really quite an astute man of business, and with Venetia's help, soon had Victor's affairs in first-rate order. Only once did she and Mr. Latimer disagree. Upon learning of the existence of Victor's open cash-box, Mr. Latimer was appalled and insisted that such a bizarre practice be discontinued immediately. To her own surprise, Venetia, who had heretofore been likewise appalled, did not agree.

"It's always been there," she said. "And I should like it to stay. It is a constant testimony to Victor's generosity and trusting nature."

"More a testimony to his foolhardiness!" Mr. Latimer grumbled.

In the end they compromised. On the first of each month the cash-box would be replenished to the amount of fifty pounds only. Mr. Latimer, however, would not be moved from his opinion that the entire idea was bird-brained.

With Jonathan installed as butler, Maggie as housekeeper, and two maids and a footman at their disposal, Venetia also found time to indulge in her own pleasures. Turner, with whom she had become quite a favourite, regularly sent a groom over with the tilbury or a riding horse, so that almost every morning she took a drive or canter in the Park. There were shopping excursions and visits to the modiste also, for Victor, rather uncharacteristically, had insisted that she must be fashionably attired. To please him, Venetia took care with her appearance, but, to own the truth, she found the constant fittings and trips for fashion accessories, which had been of such importance in her former life, rather tiresome now. She would as lief tend to the flower boxes and potted plants which she had scattered about the house or play chess and chat with Count Laurent, who had taken to dropping by two or three afternoons during the week. She was also plunging ahead with writing her romantic novel, and quite depended on Charles's opinions and advice. He had so far been impressed, and had even delighted in her ability to include humour, for which he himself had no gift.

Venetia, blushing and greatly encouraged by this praise from such an accomplished author, confided to Linda that she was tempted to give a reading in the parlour that night.

"Oh, do!" cried Linda. "'Cause it's very good, you know. And if you was to read tonight, I could be there, too." Although the agency had failed to find her a position as a housemaid, the skill with a needle which Linda had employed on making costumes for the sisters' act had finally secured her an apprenticeship with a modiste. Often she had to work at night and missed the gatherings.

By the time evening arrived, however, Venetia had become missish. "I couldn't possibly read after Charles," she contended. "My story will seem flimsy in comparison."

"Fiddle!" said Linda. "You know them novels are all the crack!" But when Venetia remained adamant, she snatched up the notebook. "Well, then, if you ain't gonna read it, I will!" she announced, and flounced out of the room.

That evening in the parlour, everyone sat in rapt attention while Charles read his latest installment. The episode was highly moving and engendered a great deal of praise. Venetia tried to catch Linda's attention and dissuade her from her course of action. But Linda, either because she did not notice or because she chose not to acknowledge Venetia, stood as soon as she had the floor.

"I got a piece for you," she said, and Venetia quaked in fearful anticipation as Linda began to read. Venetia's fear was justified insofar as Linda had taken the liberty of reading another story—one which Venetia had written soley for her own amusement. Linda launched into a lively, thinly veiled version of Venetia's own life and romantic adventures. When she came to the the part about the gypsies, everyone roared with laughter as Linda dramatically interpreted the "gypsy ritual."

Amidst the laughter Venetia looked across at Victor and realized he must have been staring at her for some time in undisguised amazement. His eyebrows shot up in the gesture which had by now become familiar to her. She could almost hear him say, "Touché!" She was unable to look away from him, and she felt a warm glow as she revelled in the sort of intimacy that they had shared that day at the gypsy camp.

Linda had completed her rendition and was now announcing the name of the new author... Venetia Allen! "Bravo!" and "Excellent!" her intimates cried as they eagerly crowded round her to offer their congratulations. Venetia was receiving an enthusiastic embrace from Charles when from over his shoulder she was startled to see a pair of hostile blue eyes fixed on her. She shuddered as she recalled Anna's warning... *She would take your treasure from you, this woman with flaxen hair!*

What treasure? Victor?

Venetia drew a quick decisive breath and thrust the nonsensical notion aside. No one could steal a treasure from her that she didn't possess. It was barely a secret that Victor was more Sally's treasure than hers. Though Victor was careful to avoid any appearance of intimacy between them, in her heart Venetia knew that on the many nights she heard him enter his bedchamber in the wee hours of the morning he had been with Sally. Nobody needed to steal what they already had.

Not that Victor's love life had anything to do with her, Venetia told herself, and refused to admit that some of the pleasure had gone out of the evening.

For himself, Victor had been flattered and vastly entertained by the budding author's obvious talent. He had had no notion she was so clever, and possessed of a delightful, wicked humour. As he started towards Venetia, he was waylaid by a tug on his sleeve. "Tonight, Victor?" Sally enquired with a purr.

"I, er, sorry. Not tonight." He drew away from Sally, leaving her too abruptly for her liking. Especially when she watched him make his way so eagerly and purposefully to Venetia—now her arch-enemy.

Upon reaching his destination, Victor grasped Venetia's hands in a gesture at once warm and intimate. His eyes sparkled as he added his compliments.

"My dear, that was delightful. Such a refreshing change from Charles's dreary story."

"By jingo, Victor, are you that fickle?" Charles asked laughing. Will you toss over a novel of serious social consequence simply to be entertained? And royally entertained, my dear," he added, kissing Venetia's hand. "Promise me you will not go public. The thought of the competition makes me quake in my boots." Shaking his head, he turned to have a word with Laurent.

"I believe you have as much talent as Charles, Venetia," said Victor. "You painted our gypsy friends in such vivid colours that I could almost see them."

"Thank you. It's kind of you to say so."

Victor was about to tell her that he had intended not only kindness but sincere praise when she glanced beyond him and quickly advised him that she must bid him good-night. "I'm engaged for an early-morning canter in the Park with Count Laurent," she said, and hastened away.

"Victor, you've been neglecting me, you know." He had not been aware of Sally's approach, and her voice beside him was both startling and provoking. Nor did he care for the tone of reproach in her voice.

"Have I?" he asked absently, ignoring the seductive message in her eyes which promised that were he to accommodate her this night, all would be forgiven.

"I can only repeat, Sally," he said evenly, "that it is not convenient tonight."

The flaxen-haired beauty held her tongue and abruptly turned her back on Victor to fawn on Count Laurent.

Chit-chat ensued amongst them all, but Victor's mind was not on what he was saying or to whom. He was unable to explain his disinclination to enjoy his mistress or his sudden compulsion to be true to his wife. Sally was willing and definitely able, while Venetia was a wife in name only. Yet she held more appeal for him than his mistress.

Not one to give up, Sally again approached him, and Victor, upon observing her hurt expression, softened. "Sally," he said by way of explanation, "so much has occurred. And so quickly. If I've been neglectful, I apologize but I—" He stopped. This was not the time to advise her of his recent pondering. "I may be engaged for some time. But soon . . . we shall see."

Sally's only answer was a knowing nod, which Victor, having again turned away, completely missed.

Charles, who had not missed it, grinned maliciously at Sally. "In a pet, puss?"

Sally simply shrugged. "Not really. I've seen this sort of thing before." She smiled confidently at him. "But as you can see, I am a woman of the world and not some untried silly chit. No cause for alarm, I assure you." She dismissed Charles by turning back to the count and imploring him to see her home, an invitation which he accepted, and with alacrity the pair bade the gathering a good-night.

Venetia had retired to her rooms some time ago, and it was too late to follow her up. A bloody good thing, too, Victor told himself, if he intended to keep to his resolve. Still, he thought wistfully, it gave him a warm feeling to know that she was nearby. And he had come to look forward to those rare evenings when the weather was inclement or there was no company and they would sit alone together in their shared sitting-room. Sometimes they engaged in a lively discussion on Charles's novel or the performance of the opera guest Hopkins had brought round the evening before. He grinned. She had such definite opinions and he enjoyed matching wits with her. But he enjoyed the quiet times, as well, when sometimes he would look up from his book and see her sitting there, reading or doing some needlework or more often poised over her notebook with quill and ink. He had thought her to be writing in her diary, the little imp! Not that he cared what she was writing. Just so long as she was there . . . her hair aglow in the flames from the fire and in their own little room made cosy and bright with her flowers and his pictures, which she had so artfully arranged.

Victor, lost in his musings, had been absently bidding his guests good-night and was almost surprised to find himself alone with Charles.

"Coming up, old boy?" asked his friend. "Or do you plan to remain here with that empty expression on your face all night?"

Victor scowled at him. "Something on my mind, is all," he grumbled.

"And I know just what it is," said Charles as, leaving Jonathan to snuff out the candles, they mounted the stairs together.

"So you've added the preternatural to your talents?"

"Not precisely." Charles grinned. "But I'll lay you a monkey you're beginning to realize that you've landed in a bed of roses when you thought you had fallen into a pile of manure."

"Take a damper, you damnable cur!" Victor said, ignoring Charles's chuckle as he turned towards his own room. But he knew what his friend was getting at. They had both initially thought Venetia a wilful, silly little chit whom Victor ought not to be forced to wed. But now they had both observed for themselves that Venetia had blossomed into a rare beauty, revealing not only a generosity of spirit but a kindness of soul and warmth of heart. Truly a diamond of the first water who was deserving of a much more suitable setting.

In spite of his numerous cautions to himself, Victor found that each day he looked forward to seeing her cheerful face across from him at the breakfast table, listening for her light footsteps on the stairs or admiring the tunes she hummed when she was happy. Entering the parlour one afternoon, he was surprised to find Venetia cosily seated over a game of chess with Count Laurent. The resentment which overwhelmed him shook him to the core. He hadn't even known she played chess!

Victor had seen the count's carriage in front of the house when he had returned from making some pur-

chases in Bond Street, and had hurried in expecting
that Laurent was waiting for him. Apparently not. As
he observed the cosy twosome, Victor was alarmed by
the fierce stab of jealousy that wrenched his heart.
Riding this morning and chess this afternoon?

Ridiculous! he told himself. Jealous of a dear friend
who was old enough to be his father? He swallowed
his pride and called out a cheerful greeting. The count,
studying the board, merely nodded, though Venetia
looked up, a welcome smile on her face.

"Victor! We were just speaking of you."

"Indeed?"

"Yes, Count Laurent was explaining how you fled
from France during the Revolution and how your
mother hid you in a barn for two whole weeks even
though you were just a boy." Her eyes held a soft look
of tender concern. "What a dreadful ordeal it must
have been for you."

"No," he said truthfully. "I was at the age, you see,
when such things were more an adventure than something to fear!"

"But were you not sad to leave France? Count
Laurent said your estate was most beautiful, with
glorious grounds and one of the best stables in the
country. Did you mind terribly coming to a strange
land?"

"Not very much," he said, also truthfully, for he
had never cared a great deal about the trappings of
wealth. "My father was already dead, you see, and my
mother travelled with me."

"Very well, Venetia!" Count Laurent broke in. "Your move. See if you are clever enough to avoid certain checkmate."

Venetia reluctantly returned her attention to the board. Victor poured himself a glass of brandy and watched the play for a minute, but his mind was quite preoccupied.

"Do you miss your home, Venetia?" he asked abruptly.

She looked up at him as if surprised by the question. "I . . . do you know, I seldom think about it anymore." Her answer seemed to surprise her, as well. "I daresay I've been much too busy to give it a thought."

"But you cannot tell me you do not miss the parties!" said the count. "And I'm going to see to it that you're reintroduced into Society where you belong, my girl! You must instruct your modiste to turn you out in the first stare of fashion, for I mean to present you next week!"

"What is this, Laurent?" Victor turned to him in surprise, the glass halfway to his lips.

"I'm hosting a ball Saturday next," said Laurent, keeping his eyes on the board. "And you and your lovely bride are to be the guests of honour."

"Yes, isn't that sweet of him, Victor?" Venetia asked.

But Victor was too busy grappling with the tumult of emotions gripping him. Who the devil did Laurent think he was! Venetia was *his* wife. It was *he* who ought to ride with her and play chess with her. *He* was a marquis, by God, and if anyone were going to present his own wife, it would be he.

The count looked up at him now, and the amused duplicity lurking in the depths of the fine grey eyes rather disconcerted Victor.

"I know that gadding about with the ton is not in your style, my boy, but Latimer has it that you might do well to do so. Good for business, don't you know?"

CHAPTER THIRTEEN

VENETIA WAS EXCITED and full of anticipation when their carriage stopped before Count Laurent's Town house. This would be her first official appearance amongst the ton since her marriage. Of course, she had encountered many of her acquaintances when she rode in the Park or shopped on Bond Street. Some had smiled and nodded, others had ignored her, but all had stared either openly or covertly. And she knew why.

But she was not troubled by either the gossip or the stares. Somehow it no longer seemed of importance to her to be accepted into their world. Perhaps it never had been. . . .

"You have no cause to be nervous, my dear," Victor said as he offered her his arm to lead her up the stairs.

"Nervous?" She looked up at him, puzzled.

"You are a properly married lady."

Dear Victor, Venetia thought. How could he know that she was not only not nervous but did not care a fig about her first social encounter. She twinkled up at him. "And I pray you will not forget it, sir! For I am married to an extremely handsome gentleman. And, unlike our wedding dinner, it appears that tonight," she said, nodding towards the plethora of carriages, "there will no no scarcity of company. I must take care that no eager lady steals you from me, for that is *de rigueur* at these functions, you must know!"

"Imp!" he said, laughing. Then he pressed her hand in encouragement. "That's my girl. Pluck to the backbone."

Venetia glanced at him as they ascended the steps. He clearly thought she was putting a brave face on it, when she had meant every word. She *was* proud to be entering this elegant Town house on his arm and just as proud to be openly acknowledged as his wife. And thusly, she lifted her head with pride as they were led up a long carpeted stairway to a landing where a footman took their wraps. Venetia instantly recognized the absence of the requisite receiving line.

"Dear me, Victor, are we late arrivals?" Venetia asked as they crossed the marbled floor and peered over a brass-filigree railing to the ballroom below, which was already swarming with guests.

"It seems we are..." he said, looking a bit puzzled. "But Laurent told me...at least I was under the impression that he wished us to arrive at precisely this hour. Perhaps we'd best go down."

As they proceeded towards the grand staircase leading to the ballroom, their progress was interrupted.

"Hello, Venetia."

Venetia turned to greet the lady but for some moments could not place her. Finally, it came to her. Eliza Sutcliffe. "Eliza! How lovely it is to see you."

But Eliza was now gazing adoringly at Victor. "You painted my portrait," she said. "And almost made me beautiful."

"You are beautiful, my dear," said the man beside her, who turned to smile at them. "And you, sir, captured Lizzie's real beauty in the portrait. How could I help but fall in love?"

"Oh, Henry!" Eliza playfully rapped her husband's hand before introducing him. "But it is quite true," she said to Venetia. "I was never really pretty until I sat for Mr. Allen. I daresay that it was his kindness that made me feel so comfortable, and perhaps that explains why I appeared prettier than I am. But from that time forward, Mr. Allen has changed my life."

Yes, Venetia thought as she listened. Victor changed everyone's life.

"And when I learned of your elopement ... Oh!" Eliza covered her mouth with her hand! "Oh, I do beg your pardon. I only meant I thought you to be a very lucky woman. Please accept my felicitations and my very best wishes for a happy future together," she finished in frank sincerity.

"Thank you, Eliza. I cannot think of a lovelier way to begin the evening!" Venetia said.

At the top of the grand staircase Victor placed his card on the salver of the footman, who then announced the couple in loud ringing tones, "The Marquis and Marchioness de Beauchante."

Venetia glanced quickly at Victor, but he was staring in astonishment at the footman, who had turned to receive the next guests' card. Venetia tugged at Victor's sleeve. "Come along. We are in the way."

"Strange," he said. "My card simply announced me as Victor Allen. How could he have known?" Victor mused aloud as he accompanied Venetia down the staircase to the ballroom.

The mischievous glint in Count Laurent's eyes instantly alerted Victor to the culprit.

"You old reprobate!" Victor admonished him. "You know I discarded all that rot long ago."

"Look here, Victor," the count said as he gestured to a guest who was summoning him. "It don't hurt to advertise, do it?"

Venetia had no notion whether Victor's portrait business would increase, but his newly disclosed title seemed to be excessively improving their social standing. The haughty disapproving stares to which she had previously been subjected had quite suddenly changed to stares of amazement and acceptance. The tabbies of the ton were perishing to gossip with her rather than about her, and she and Victor were besieged by all who could get near them. Venetia, enveloped in a flurry of former friends and mere acquaintances eager to establish an intimate relationship, found herself separated from Victor, who was also coping with a newly found popularity. It was Emma who finally managed to pull Venetia away to a small alcove where they could be private.

"Oh, Venetia, I've been dying to see you!" Emma had just returned from her wedding trip and was not even aware that Venetia had been located, much less married. "No one even sent us word on the Continent, and we were away so long. But I knew all along where you had got to.''

"But how could you have?" asked Venetia. She had not even known herself where she would go.

"You peagoose! Do you think me blind or deaf? Victor Allen was the only thing you spoke about from the very instant you first set eyes upon him. It was plain as a pikestaff to me that you were heel over ears in love with him. Oh, it is too romantic. But you never said he was a marquis!''

"I—I didn't know.''

"I wager that if your parents had known that they'd not have fled to Farsdale. Your papa put it about that he was required there on urgent matters, but my mama declares it was to escape the gossip. You should have told them Victor was a marquis, Venetia, and I daresay they would have been just as happy to marry you to Victor and send you off with a proper wedding.''

"No, Emma, I don't think..." Venetia hesitated, her feelings jumbled. Emma clearly thought that she had all along intended to flee to Gretna Green with Victor. Should she correct her friend's misapprehension? And what of her parents? Would it be different between them now that she was a marchioness?

"At any rate, I cannot fault you, Venetia.''

"Fault me?''

"Oh, no. I can see that Victor Allen is everything you said he was. And so handsome, too! How could you help falling in love with him! Oh, there's Mama beckoning to me. You must tell me everything later,'' Emma said, and hurried away.

Venetia stared after her, her head in a spin. In love? With Victor? The thought struck her like a thunderbolt, and her gaze quickly sought him out. She spotted him across the room, engaged in a conversation with Lord Dutton and Lady Axley. Victor, always self-assured and self-possessed, was as much at ease among this elegant company as he had been among the gypsies. She watched as he bent his head slightly to listen to whatever Lady Axley was saying as intently as he would listen to Oliver, the little errand boy. He did not discrimate, for that was not in Victor's character. Yes, he was unpredictable and volatile at times, but he was ever kind. She was certainly fond of him, but...love? Did she...?

"Venetia," said a voice that seemed familiar. "Or perhaps I should properly address you as 'my lady'?" Venetia turned to discover the reason why the voice was so familiar. She struggled to control her reeling senses.

"Bertram, Your Grace, how...lovely to see you" was all she could think to say to the man who had once been the centre of her life. And whom she had completely forgotten.

"I did not expect to receive such unladylike behaviour from you, Venetia!" he said, his grey eyes seeming to rake over every inch of her, from the red hair piled high on her head to the satin emerald slippers that matched the soft crepe gown that bared her shoulders and clung so provocatively to her slender figure.

"I hardly think that was the proper way to cry off, my sweet."

"I had meant to write you a note, Bertram." Her conscience smote her. "But Papa advised against it since he did not believe there to be a proper way. I am sorry. I did not think," she said feeling discomfitted and embarrassed. "Did Papa return your ring as I asked him to?" she enquired, trying to dispel the tension.

"Ah, yes, the ring," said Bertram. "He did, but nothing could heal my broken heart."

That, indeed, was doing it a bit too brown. Venetia's head jerked up and her eyes flashed. Then she remembered where she was and smiled sweetly as she said, "Come now, Your Grace. Let us not pretend that your heart was engaged. Surely you would find it easy to replace a silly chit of a girl who was only required to supply you with an heir? I am certain it did not diminish the ardent passions you and your *chère amie* shared for so many years!"

"Venetia!" The duke's grey eyes widened in horror as well as surprise. But his expression changed to one of relief and earnestness as he was finally able to comprehend the meaning of her sudden departure from his life. "Good Lord, Venetia!" he began as he shook his head. "You must know that men have certain, shall we say, weaknesses. But that did not mean I did not adore you, for I did. Still do, in fact. Blast your eyes, Venetia," he said in exasperation. "Why did you not speak to me first before destroying our future?" He moved closer to her, and said in a beseeching voice, "It is not too late, my love. I shall fix everything."

But Venetia had ceased to listen and was glad to be approached by Lord Bottomly, who was of sufficient intimacy with the duke to give him a curt nod of dismissal.

"My dear," said that foppish gentleman, "Hazlemere has monopolized you quite long enough. Come, let me get a glass of champagne for you."

Graciously extending her hand and bestowing a warm smile on Bertram, she gladly allowed Lord Bottomly to lead her away. She chuckled with him as he congratulated her upon "giving the gossip-mongers yet another on-dit to chew on." She did not know that Victor had witnessed her encounter with Bertram. Nor did she realize that the gracious manner she had so carefully cultivated to contend with the duplicitous duke had been subject to misinterpretation.

Yes, Victor had seen them together and had not been best pleased. While Venetia had been all that was proper, he had detected in her manner a certain furtiveness, or was that forgiveness? And as for the duke... There had been no mistaking the gleam in his eyes. The gleam of ardent, undiminished desire. Was this then the love that could not die? She could so easily be his wife, Victor thought, here in the setting where she belonged. If she could gracefully be rid of me, he added, and felt a painful lurch in his heart.

AFTER THIS spectacular entrance back into Society for the marquis and his marchioness, the invitations poured in. Some Victor accepted, many he did not. For all intents and purposes, he remained simply Victor Allen. But Mr. Latimer did not hesitate to put it widely about that his client, the Marquis de Beauchante, formerly known only as Victor Allen, was indeed the painter of a variety of notable portraits. Victor's appointment book was soon filled with dates for sittings beyond the year's end. And it was only mid-summer. This windfall was due mainly to the overdue recognition of Victor's considerable talents as well as to his greatly improved status amongst Society. The latter aspect was the one on which Mr. Latimer traded, together with a considerable raise in the rate of commissions.

Although Victor seldom attended Society functions himself, he was always eager for Venetia to do so. Venetia, assuming that Victor was loath to puff up his consequence to better his business, did make frequent appearances escorted by the count. But, to own the truth, she herself was equally reluctant, for she found her evenings at home much more enjoyable and rewarding.

What she missed most, though she tried to deny it, were the evenings alone with Victor in their shared sitting-room. But even they were becoming rare, almost as if he were deliberately avoiding her. Or perhaps seeking more exciting company? She would not admit, even to herself, how much that thought disturbed her.

SALLY HAD NOT been surprised to find Victor's interest waning, but she knew he was only temporarily besotted with the youthful beauty of his bride, and decided it was best to let him have his head. It was only a matter of time before he tired of his new toy and returned to her true blue arms.

Meanwhile, though Victor's interest might have waned, his generosity had not. He had recently settled upon her a tidy sum, which Sally, always with an eye to the future, had safely put away. He had added that she was as welcome as always to whatever funds she required. That being so, she directed her footsteps to Fitzroy Square, for she had in mind something quite special that would appeal to Lord Ashley. A woman in her position must always be prepared. She entered the house and went directly up to Victor's garret. She breezily greeted Jonathan.

"Hello, Jonathan," she said, reaching into the box.

"Good afternoon, Miss Ellerby," he replied, inclining his head.

Sally paused with her hand in the box, as she discovered it was all but empty. There could not be more than four pounds altogether. Not nearly enough.

Hiding her irritation, she turned around to question the butler. "Jonathan, where's Victor?"

"I really couldn't say, Miss Ellerby. He left above an hour ago."

"Oh, drat!" If she delayed too long, that fetching little hat would be gone. "This is most unusual," she mused aloud. "Why is this box almost empty?"

"I think," said Jonathan politely, "that her ladyship thought it prudent to limit funds likely to be needlessly squandered by recipients of his lordship's overindulgence."

Sally turned sharply. Was there a hint of malice in the man's tone? But Jonathan's face belied no hostility as he carefully set out a brush to dry.

Sally was incensed. Her ladyship, indeed! Well, no little Miss Prunes and Prisms, Quality or no Quality, was going to put a rub in her way, she fumed. Turning on her heel, she descended the steps in a fury.

Venetia, pruning a large plant in the entry hall, turned at the sound of footsteps on the stairs. "Hello, Sally," she said. "I did not see you come in."

"Venetia! Where is Victor?" Sally demanded, neglecting to return her greeting.

Venetia, at first stunned by the rudeness in Sally's tone, was struck speechless. Then, in a sudden flash of anger, she quickly shot back, "I do not know, Miss Ellerby, and if I did, why should I tell you?"

"Then you will kindly tell him for me that there was not enough blunt in the box to cover my purchases today... thanks to you!" Sally hissed. "And you can also tell him that I will take them on tick and have them put it on his tab."

Before Venetia could manage a response, Sally strutted through the hall and sped out of the front door, down the front steps and onto Fitzroy Square.

Venetia, fully furious and more than a little puzzled, looked up at Jonathan, who had followed Sally down. "What ever did she mean 'take it on tick' and 'put it on his tab'?"

The corner of Jonathan's mouth twitched ever so slightly. "I apprehend, your ladyship, that it is her intention to make certain purchases, the bills of which will be directed to Mr. Allen."

Venetia's eyes widened and she felt her nails bite into her palms. Startled, she stared down at her clenched fists.

"Thank you, Jonathan," she said quietly as she dusted the dried leaves from her hand. "As soon as Mr. Allen returns, will you please inform him that I would like to speak with him immediately."

She mounted the steps and swept by him. Once in her sitting-room, she slammed the door with a bang!

I will not have it! I will not! she fumed. *I knew her for what she was the first time I saw her. And I saw how she pulled on Victor! Oh, men are such fools!* She walked to the mantel and gripped it hard with both hands. Then she turned quickly and spoke aloud. "Well, Victor, you are my husband now. And I will not have this abandoned woman who carries your favour make a cake of me! I will not!"

Unable to contain herself, Venetia took several turns about the room. Then, jolted by a stab of memory, she stopped. *An enemy...a woman with flaxen hair...she would take your treasure from you.*

Venetia pressed her hands to her hot cheeks. She had to be calm. Perhaps if she were able to distract herself...

Deliberately picking up the book she had most recently been reading, she settled herself on the sofa. She read and reread a single page but saw not one line of print. The only thing she saw was Victor's image. Victor's glowing face as he laughed at her silly stories. Victor's flashing eyes as he scolded her. Victor's passionate expression as he bent to tenderly kiss Sally.

Sally! A sharp pain wrenched Venetia from her reverie. She tossed the book aside and resumed pacing. Where was he? It was very near dawn. She knew he eschewed his club and loathed playing cards.

Venetia tried to shut out the images of her husband lying in the arms of her flaxen-haired enemy. But she couldn't.

Her fingers grasped the first thing to hand, and the tiny crystal vase struck the fireplace, shattering into bits. Appalled at herself, Venetia looked down at the rosebud lying amongst the slivers of glass and the spilled water. *"Fool!"* she cried, not knowing whether she meant Victor or herself.

CHAPTER FOURTEEN

I HATE CARDS, Victor thought as he fumbled, unsuccessfully trying to turn the handle of his own front door. Dull as dishwater. Sitting for hours in a smoke-filled room with a bunch of starched shirts with rheumy eyes and greedy hands who disavowed any interest in the outcome of the game. While most of them or all of them were deep in dun territory. Hah! The Quality! Damn, but he was as drunk as an emperor.

Ah! He smiled as he at last caught the slippery door handle and turned it. He entered the house, quietly shut the door and unsteadily made his way up the stairs.

A dead bore. He'd much rather have spent the evening in the sitting-room with Venetia, basking in the glow of her beautiful... He shook his head, trying to banish her image from his mind. If he avoided her... stayed away... he could keep his resolve. He did not even glance towards her door as he made his way to his own bedchamber.

Bosky as he was, and boots being what they were, he struggled, accompanied by a string of oaths, until at last they hit the floor with a resounding thud. His feet were bare and he was perched on his bed attempting to unbutton his shirt when his door flew open.

"I know the hour is late... or I should say early!" Venetia's lips curled derisively. "But I have been waiting all evening to speak with you and I will not wait any longer!"

"Oh?" Victor hardly heard what had been said, so engrossed was he by the vision before him. Venetia. The delicious curves of her slender body seductively outlined in a heavenly creation of transparent silk and lace. Her hair, glowing like banked coals in the pool of his candle, tumbled to her waist. He had not noticed it was so long. He wanted to—

"This has gone on long enough and I insist that we come to an understanding tonight!"

"Yes, of course." Victor rose unsteadily to his feet and tried to clear his muddled brain. Had she said she'd been waiting to speak to him all evening? "I didn't know," he faltered. "I would have returned earlier. I was just—"

"Where you have been is of course not my affair," she said with asperity. "But I must remind you that you are my husband!"

"Of course," he said again, his eyes on her heaving bosom. Yes, by gad, he was her husband!

"And I must inform you... no, I insist upon it! It is my place... not Sally's... to run your... our household!"

"What... has Sally to say to anything?" he asked, his senses confused by the enticing sight of her cleavage. He moved towards her, consumed by a urgent desire to—

"You know full well what I am referring to! Your precious Miss Ellerby was here today with instructions to advise you that she meant you to go on paying her bills. And she was most definite in her complaints about certain changes I saw fit to make.'' Venetia's voice was almost shrill in her outrage and pain.

He was alarmed by the genuine distress so apparent in her eyes. ''You need not plague yourself over Sally, my dear. I have recently seen her and arranged everything,'' he said reassuringly.

She glared at him as if still dissatisfied with his answer, though truthfully, she was not certain of his meaning. ''Well,'' she said. ''I trust then that Sally will know her place. After all, I am your wife!''

''Mais oui, ma chérie,'' he said huskily as he brushed back a lock of her glorious hair. Troubled by the look of uncertainty in her eyes, he tried to soothe her. ''Don't be so sad, Venetia. You are my lady. You and no one else will run my household.''

''Oh, I see. Your household! Just like any housekeeper,'' she said, her eyes flashing. ''But—'' She stopped, biting her lower lip.

''Yes?'' he prompted, gently stroking her satiny cheek.

''Nothing.'' She turned away. But he could not let her go, this lovely desirable woman who was his wife and whom he wanted as he had never before wanted any woman. He caught her hand, urging her back.

''Would you like to be more than a housekeeper to me, Venetia?'' he asked, his thumb gently caressing the palm of her hand.

She drew a quick intake of breath and swallowed. ''What . . . whatever do you mean?''

"I daresay you know what I mean, my sweet," he said, bending to kiss the soft palm.

The touch of his lips against her skin wakened a warm yearning deep inside her and she wished... She abruptly pulled her hand away. "How dare you tease me! I am not a mistress!" She looked into his eyes so dark with passion and wished not for the first time since she'd met Victor that she knew how to pleasure a man.

"You do not know it yet, but you are a very desirable woman, Venetia," he said huskily as he enfolded her in his arms and tenderly kissed her temple. "And you are my wife. Would you like to truly become my wife?" he asked, tracing light kisses along her cheek and nibbling at her ear.

"I—I don't know," she whispered, feeling her knees weaken and her body becoming consumed by a raw ache. Oh, yes, she did want...

"Let me make you happy, my love..." he whispered, and Venetia's whole being pulsated with a throbbing desire as his mouth descended to caress the racing pulse at the base of her throat. "Shall I truly make you mine, my sweet?"

"Oh, Victor...oh, yes...I..." Her voice faltered and she wound her arms tightly around his neck, her fingers tangling in his hair as she pressed closer to him. He untied her negligee and let it fall to the floor.

"You are so very beautiful, my darling. I love and want to love you with all my heart," he whispered as he began to stroke her most intimately. Venetia felt no shame, only ardent waves of pleasure and desire as her

nightgown crumpled at her feet and Victor carried her
to his bed.

VENETIA AWAKENED late the next morning, a smile
curving her lips. Nothing in Mrs. Radcliffe's novels
had prepared her for the joy, the ecstasy and the passionate fulfillment of the coupling with her darling
Victor. Victor. So gentle yet powerful. She turned in
the bed to instinctively reach for him and was disappointed to find him gone. Drowsily, she propped herself up on her elbow and surveyed the unfamiliar
room. Bright sunlight was filtering through the draperies that had not yet been opened. Her gaze fell on
Victor's dressing table, laid upon which were a set of
silver brushes. She sighed and turned her head to see
a note propped against the candlestick on the bedside
table. She reached for it in eager anticipation.

Venetia,
Sorry... an early appointment at Hilton Head.
Likely to be gone for the entire day but will join
you at dinner.

V

Her instinctive response was disappointment. The
note contained none of the endearments he had murmured so passionately last night.

But she firmly thrust aside her momentary unhap-
piness, for she knew it was, after all, a hastily scrib-
bled note, but significant just the same. For the first
time, Victor had apprised her of his whereabouts because he wished her to know. As any husband would

wish his wife to know. His *true* wife. Venetia felt the blood rush to her cheeks as a warm glow of happiness suffused her.

She lay back upon the bed and reached for Victor's pillow. Breathing in the sweet scents of brandy, tobacco and the essence of Victor, she hugged the pillow to her and fell asleep again.

ASTRIDE TURNER'S black stallion, Victor, riding hard to meet his appointment, wrestled with his conscience. He had seduced his own wife and had broken his resolve, robbing her of everything she so richly deserved.

He had not meant to. Having faced the fact that he had fallen hopelessly in love with her, he had for the past several weeks purposely avoided her.

But when she had entered his room last night . . . so entrancing, so utterly desirable, he had completely lost his control. He was only human and he had wanted her more than ever before. He could no more have stopped himself than he could have stopped breathing. Making love to Venetia had been unlike anything he had ever experienced with any other woman. His mother had had a very simple answer for it. She had said, "If ever you fall in love, my son, really in love, you will know!"

And now, by gad, he knew! No woman other than Venetia would ever satisfy him. When he had awakened at dawn this morning with her cradled in his arms, her silky hair trailing across his chest, it was all he could do not to make love to her again. To feel her arms tight about him, to hear her little cries of pleasure . . .

Oh, yes, her response had been like an excitation to his already aroused senses. If she had not seemed so willing, even eager, as if she too loved him . . . No, he thought, for that was nothing more than wishful thinking. The simple fact had been that he had wanted her and had induced her to want him. Oh, yes, he knew well how to tempt a woman, how to awaken the erotic passions even in a woman as sweet and innocent as his virgin Venetia. Until last night, he amended.

Gad! He had ruined her! How could he have thought it possible to live under the same roof as Venetia and never so much as touch her for three whole years and now . . . Perhaps, in time, she could come to love him.

Fool, he told himself as he turned the stallion onto the driveway leading into Lord Jamieson's vast Hilton Head estate. Once again, Victor thought of how much more Venetia was suited to such a setting. Hazlemere must have above a half-dozen such estates. Did she love the duke? It had not been many weeks ago that she had come running to him, sobbing as if her heart were broken. But hearts do not break, they sting and ache . . . and are easily repaired when one's beloved returns.

Divorce was not an impossibility, for scandals die away.

At the manor house he dismounted and made his way up the steps to the front door. Yes, he thought as he looked back at the carefully manicured gardens.

Venetia would be happy in a setting such as this. He
had promised Lord Jamieson that he would come to
his estate to do a portrait of his wife. He preferred to
work in his own garret where there was always plenty
of natural light, but Lady Jamieson was confined to
home owing to a recent indisposition and it might not
be such a bad thing for Victor to be away from
home....

WHEN ASKED, Jonathan advised Venetia that Hilton
Head was some distance away and that Victor would
probably be late returning. She ordered dinner put
back. She was glad there would be no company tonight and that both Charles and Linda were elsewhere engaged. It would be pleasant to enjoy a quiet,
intimate dinner alone with Victor. After last night...
Her colour rose again as she relived the memory and
she awaited his arrival in a fever of longing and anticipation.

Geraniums from the front window-boxes, along
with a few sprays of fern from a potted plant, made a
lovely centrepiece, which she placed on the dinner table between two brass candlesticks. She dressed carefully in a gown of shimmering silk gauze with a
décolletage too low for an informal evening at home.
But Victor had once admired her in it and had said the
colour exactly matched her eyes. She instructed Bella
to prepare Victor's favourite dishes and requested
Jonathan to chill a bottle of champagne. Then she selected a book and retreated to the small withdrawing-
room to wait. She didn't mind that dinner was to be

late, for she was too full of nervous excitement to think of eating.

"Madam," Jonathan announced. "It is past eight. Bella has advised me that the roast is drying out and wondered if perhaps you might like to have your dinner now." Seeing her glance at the clock, he cleared his throat. "It's quite possible, my lady, that Mr. Allen was delayed at Hilton Head and may have been invited to dine there."

"I expect you're right," she said, and reluctantly entered the dining-room alone. But she had little appetite for the delicious meal Bella had prepared, and as soon as was proper, she retreated again to the withdrawing-room and her book. But she was alert to every sound that might signal Victor's arrival, and when a few minutes later she heard a carriage stop in front of the house she stood up and laid her book aside. Her expression fell as Jonathan and not Victor entered the room. Almost apologetically, Jonathan extended to her a salver with a calling card.

She took the card from the tray. Bertram. What on earth was he doing here at this hour? she wondered. It was nearly nine. However, she advised Jonathan that she would receive the duke in the parlour. Jonathan admitted that he had already shown the gentleman to that room.

The Duke of Hazlemere stood in the parlour and stared up at the portrait over the mantel. It was obviously of Venetia, but not of the Venetia he knew. She was posed holding on to a mongrel, with her head thrown back in laughter, while her hair, held back feebly by a colourful scarf, fell about her face in abandoned disarray. But the more he looked, the more he recognized her. There in her eyes was the same sparkle of mischief that had drawn him to her that very first night. He had known then that of all the debutantes, no other could hold his interest.

And still did. Though she had insulted both his rank and integrity, Hazlemere had determined to forgive her. He felt certain now that she had not married Allen for love and felt equally certain that with the right inducements, she would be more than willing to return to him.

"Ah! Venetia, my dear," he said with reverence as she entered the parlour. Indeed, she was intoxicatingly beautiful, and his eyes roamed to the enticing décolletage of her silky gown. Yet when he met her eyes, he felt a sudden jolt. There was something about her glowing colour, and the contentment in her lovely face... Almost as if she had blossomed overnight. Could he have been mistaken about this marriage? Could she possibly be in love with a mere paint-pusher?

"Your Grace," she said, extending her hand.

"Come now, Venetia," he said, taking the proffered hand and bending over it. "Must you address me in that formal fashion? Once it was Bertram."

"That, your lordship, was under different circumstances and some time ago."

"Then, for old times' sake, let us not be formal. As a matter of fact, that is why I came tonight. I thought perhaps I could persuade you to ride with me in the Park tomorrow morning. I have a spirited little filly

I'd like you to try. And we could renew our acquaintance, so to speak.''

The gorgeous green eyes registered surprise. "Thank you. That is indeed kind of you, Your Grace. But I must beg off. I—I am dreadfully busy these days.''

"Not too busy, I apprehend, to forgo early-morning gallops in the Park several times a week. Oh, yes, you have drawn notice, my dear. Surely a canter with me would do little harm?''

Venetia frowned, trying to form another excuse while wondering why Bertram had really come and why he did not simply leave. And where was Victor?

VICTOR DISMOUNTED and paid off the groom who was to take the stallion back to Turner's stable. Then he studied the smart phaeton in front of his house, the perfectly matched bays, the crest on the panel proclaiming it to be Hazlemere's. So, it seemed he had been correct. He swallowed the lump in his throat and entered his house.

"Victor!" Venetia turned a glowing face to him as he strode into the parlour.

"I am sorry to be late," he said, bowing with cool civility over her hand. "I was delayed. I see you have a visitor.'' He turned to the duke. "How do you do, Your Grace?''

"Very well, thank you," said the Duke, who had been watching the two of them with interest. "I came down hoping I could persuade Lady Allen to ride with me in the Park tomorrow morning. I have a particular horse that I should very much like her to try.''

"Splendid!" said Victor. "I suppose you know she's an excellent rider. You have been remiss, Venetia. Have you not offered your guest refreshments? Pray be seated, Your Grace, and let me pour you a glass of Madeira."

"Oh, yes, do," Venetia said quickly. "I was so... that is, I had not expected company."

"Madeira, my dear?" Victor asked. She shook her head and Victor poured for himself and the duke. "It is indeed kind of you to seat her, Your Grace. She deserves better than that hack of Turner's."

"Victor, that is not at all true!" Venetia cried. "Tinker's a fine mare."

"Undoubtedly," said Victor. "But surely not to be compared with one of the duke's Thoroughbreds. I'd like to see you cut a dash, my dear, on a horse deserving of your skill. I insist that you accept the duke's kind offer."

"Oh, I...very well." Venetia stared at Victor. Why was he urging her to ride with Bertram? And why was he being so distant and cool? She wished they were alone so she could speak to him, but the duke showed no signs of leave-taking.

Nor did Victor press him to do so. In fact, quite the opposite. He settled comfortably into his chair, crossed his legs and engaged the duke in a lengthy discussion about one of his bloods that had recently won at Epsom. From there, the two of them went on to project the performance of the duke's best contenders against the new crop of competition. By the time the duke made signs of departure Venetia was beside herself.

She reassured him yet again that she would be pleased to ride with him at eight and that his invitation was most kind.

When at last Jonathan showed the duke out, she turned to Victor.

"Are you certain I ought to accompany Bertram tomorrow?" she asked, feeling awkward both for having to pose the question and because his behaviour was so confusing.

"Of course you should, my dear. After all, you almost married him," he said nonchalantly. As they ascended the stairs together, he added that since he was apt to be engaged at Hilton Head a great deal during the next several days, perhaps the duke could be persuaded to keep company with her.

Venetia was silent, listening for some clue as to why Victor had become such a stranger to her. But as they entered their sitting-room she was certain he would drop the charade to take her in his arms again.

"Venetia," he said, closing the door. "I—I must beg your forgiveness. Last night…I was a bit… I was out of line to force my attentions upon you."

"But, Victor, you didn't—"

"I promise you it will not happen again. Can you ever forgive me?"

He might as well have slapped her.

"Of…of course," she said when she could manage to speak.

"Thank you." He pressed her hand but turned away as if he could not bear to look at her. "It has been a long day for us both. Good night, my dear."

She stared at his closed door with an overwhelming sense of numbness. But had he not just last night told her that he loved her? Had he not been loving and gentle as he had gently and passionately initiated her into the glories of womanhood?

Venetia suddenly went cold as she was struck force-ably by an undeniable truth. Victor had long since been initiated himself, and what was new and thrilling for her might very well not have been the same for him.

Was that what he had been too kind to say? That she did not please him?

Pressing her hand to her mouth as if to force back the hurt and despair that struggled to be heard, she entered her chamber and sank onto the bed. No, she hadn't pleased him, she thought. How could she when Sally knew far more and better than ever she could how to pleasure her husband?

She almost laughed at the irony of it all. She had run away to escape marrying a man who kept a mistress. And now she was married to one whose mistress ran tame under her roof!

Well, she would not run away from Victor! She loved him. And she would not let Sally have him!

She sat up, sobered by the hot fury which possessed her.

"She shan't have him!" Venetia declared aloud. And one shoe flung hard against the wall stamped her determination!

CHAPTER FIFTEEN

THE ESSENTIAL DIFFICULTY, Venetia soon determined, was that she did not in the least know how to entice a man even if that man was her husband. The next difficulty proved to be that she never saw him, for Victor, if not shut up in his garret, seemed always to be away from home.

Perhaps he had returned to the welcoming and more experienced arms of his mistress. Well, Venetia fumed, what was sauce for the gander was sauce for the goose. Had he not encouaged her to seek out the company of the duke?

In the weeks that followed, Venetia accepted every invitation she received and was soon involved in a whirlwind of social activity. More and more often she accepted the escort of the duke and sometimes another former suitor. Bertram, however, was the most persistent. And, to own the truth, she found his company diverting and his attentions flattering after Victor's open rejection. His manners were easy and engaging and he made a delightful companion at a soirée or at the theatre. And she did enjoy the now regular morning rides in the Park, mounted on one of his prize horses.

But soon enough the novelty paled and so did Bertram.

Bertram was not Victor.

And her scheme was not working, Venetia thought in a fit of despondency. Though she was careful to see that Victor was always informed of her whereabouts and openly flirted with Bertram in order that Victor should hear of it at every opportunity, he was not at all affected. He had only vaguely smiled when over breakfast one morning she had raved about Bertram's expertise with the whip. Indeed Victor seemed hardly aware of her new popularity, much less aroused to a fever of jealousy over it!

Had she but known it, Victor was keenly aware of her every move. What he did not gain from her he solicited from the count.

"Yes, she is at Crockers' grand ball tonight and escorted, I believe, by the Duke of Hazlemere," confirmed the count that evening. He shifted his attention from the chessboard to give Victor a speculative look. "As a notably neglectful husband, my friend, you exhibit a remarkably excessive curiosity about your wife's activities."

Victor shrugged. He had divulged nothing of his plan to the count. One never knew if one would be successful. "My only interest is that she enjoy herself," he said.

"Seems to be," said the count, his hand hovering over a knight. "Centre of the latest on-dit."

"Oh?" Victor said, feigning disinterest. "How so?"

"Bets on the book at White's. Will she or will she not replace Lady Beatrice?"

Victor was hit as if by a bolt of lightning, and the chess pieces swam before his eyes. As the duke's mistress! Never! That anyone could even think it of Venetia caused his head to throb dangerously.

"Well, now that was a stupid move," said Laurent. "You walked right into my trap! Checkmate!"

"Ah, yes, so I see," said Victor, staring blankly at the board. By gad, he'd have a word with Hazlemere! "Do you mind if we call it a night, sir? I've a rather heavy schedule tomorrow."

"Not at all, my boy. I could do with an extra wink or two myself," said the count, a smile of satisfaction on his face.

VICTOR STOOD in the duke's drawing-room, his riding whip tapping a rapid tattoo against his leg. How did one go about asking a man if his intentions towards your wife were honourable?

"Good afternoon, my lord," said the duke as he came into the room. "This is indeed a pleasant surprise."

"Good afternoon, Your Grace," Victor replied, and then proceeded without preamble. "I am informed that my wife's name is on the betting book at White's."

"And you came to call me out?" asked the Duke quite amiably.

"I came to make sure we understand each other."

"Good!" said the duke, gesturing towards a chair. "Pray be seated and let us have our chat over brandy. Or do you prefer port?"

"Brandy is fine," said Victor, but he did not sit down. It seemed he felt on firmer ground when on his feet. "Thank you." He took the glass, laying his riding whip on a low table. "You have been seeing a good deal of my wife, Your Grace."

"I had the impression that it was with your unqualified approval."

"Not precisely unqualified."

"Oh?" The duke rested against the edge of his desk and looked at Victor over his glass.

"I don't like my wife's name on a betting book."

"My dear fellow, my rank places me in the unenviable position of having my every move scrutinized by every prattle-box in Town. It is only inevitable that the excitement over my next move would result in a wager."

"I don't like the tone of this wager."

"I see." The duke gazed at his drink with some intensity. "Are you by any chance questioning the nature of my intentions?"

"That is precisely what I am doing," Victor answered severely.

"The question seems to place you more in the role of father protector than husband."

"Just so."

The duke smiled. "I had gathered as much."

"Perhaps prematurely," Victor said quickly. "I assure you that we are quite thoroughly married. Venetia is a lady."

"I never doubted it. A lady who would beautifully grace my several estates."

"Then we understand each other," said Victor.

"Indeed. I take it you are amenable to divorce?"

"If it could be arranged without scandal."

"My dear fellow, my rank also places me in a position to see that my wealth is distributed to, shall we say, the most appropriate of persons. There will be no scandal."

"I would rather agree and hope not. Then we do indeed understand each other," said Victor with a nod. "Thank you for the drink. And I'll take my leave."

AS THE DUKE handed her down from his carriage, Venetia glanced up at her house. They had returned rather early from the theatre. Would she surprise Victor at home?

"Do you mind if I come in for a moment, my dear? There is something I wish to discuss with you."

"Certainly, Bertram. Please do." Venetia felt it best they should speak, for she also had something to discuss with him.

The night was chilly, and she was glad to see there was still a fire burning steadily in the grate as they entered the quiet parlour. She summoned Jonathan to bring her tea. "And His Grace will have . . . brandy?" she asked the duke.

"I will take tea with you, my lady," he said, moving towards the fire and gazing up at her portrait. "This painting of you is quite extraordinary."

"Yes. It was done by my husband." She had been glad when the count purchased it from the gallery and presented it to her. Victor had no conceit about his accomplishments. Always intensely absorbed in whatever he was painting, he lost interest as soon as it was completed and he had blithely allowed Latimer to sell every one of the gypsy paintings. Had he discarded the memory of that bright happy day, as well?

"He has certainly caught your expression, Venetia. But the setting..." He turned to her. "Your father tells me that Allen was painting a portrait of you when...which was intended for me," he finished. "Where is it?"

"I—I don't know." Likely he had stored it away with the rest of his discards, she thought. Her papa had never taken delivery of it.

"I'd like to purchase it."

"Oh, no, I'd rather you didn't," she said quickly. "It was so formal, you see, as it was to...meant..." she faltered.

"Meant to be hung in my family's gallery, I apprehend," he finished for her.

She blushed and was relieved to see Jonathan enter with the tea tray. She retreated to the sofa and busied herself with the pouring out.

"You were wrong to run from me, Venetia," he said, taking the cup she offered to him.

"I'm sorry," she said untruthfully, feeling suddenly hemmed in.

"I would have mended my ways, Venetia. And we are so perfectly suited. It would have been a happy union."

"Perhaps," she said thoughtfully. If she had never met Victor.

He set down his cup and sat beside her. "We could still be united, my dear. You must know that I am madly in love with you?"

"Your Grace!" said Venetia, much alarmed. "Bertram, of course I am flattered by your persistence, but I had this night decided that I must tell you that while I have enjoyed your company, I think it best we—"

"No, Venetia," he said, taking her hand. "You shall not run away from me again."

She snatched her hand away. "Please. We must end this discussion."

"No, I can no longer admire you from a distance. You must know how much I want you."

"As your new mistress?" she hissed. "How dare you insult me so!"

Bertram chuckled and squeezed her hand. "My poor darling. You misunderstand me. I'm asking you to be my wife."

"Your wife?" She stared at him in astonishment. "That is impossible. I am married to Victor Allen."

"There is such a thing as divorce, my dear."

"Now you are speaking fustian," she said, picking up her cup to prevent him from again taking her hand. "I do value your friendship, Bertram. And I would not for all the world involve you in a dreadful scandal."

He shrugged. "A small scandal does not signify. I've spoken to my solicitor and he has it that with Allen's cooperation—"

"Cooperation? Victor? What are you saying?"

"That you need have no fear on that score. I have discussed it with your husband and he is amenable."

"You have discussed... And he..." The blood pounded against her temple and she took several deep breaths. Carefully she replaced her cup on the table and stood up. Unable to stand still, she moved rapidly towards the fireplace. "How dare he!" she cried in outrage.

"My dear, calm yourself," said the duke, following her. "Allen's only concern is for your happiness. He is aware how much you long to be back amongst your own set. To enjoy the society and consequence that suits you."

"Victor said that?"

"Of course...in effect. He knows as well as I that this—" his gaze flicked towards her portrait, then swept around the room "—is not the proper setting for you!"

Venetia stared at him blankly, her mind in a whirl, a tumult of hurt, rage and humiliation seething within her! She could barely believe Victor had plotted such a dastardly deed to rid himself of her!

"You belong at Lynderly," the duke was saying, "with your portrait hanging in my gallery." He spoke in eloquent terms about what a beautiful duchess she would make, the long wedding trip they would take, and their glorious return to his manicured gardens, his various estates, and how happy he would make her.

But Venetia hardly heard him. Instead she heard only Victor's voice saying on that fateful night, "Let me make you happy..."

She was startled when the duke pulled her into his arms. "Oh, my darling, you have only to say yes."

"No, Bertram, stop. Please say no more." She pushed away from him. "I am fond of you, Bertram. And I appreciate . . . am conscious of the honour you do me. But I could never . . . never leave Victor. I love him. And now, pray excuse me." She fled from the room, choked by the rage and hurt that consumed her and never saw the look of profound astonishment on his face.

VICTOR, WHO WAS UNAWARE that Venetia had returned, gave a start when she burst into the sitting-room and slammed the door behind her.

"Oh, Venetia. I was not expecting you," he said, looking up from his book. "Rather early to return, isn't it?" Then, seeing the dagger-like flash of fury in her eyes and the unmistakable quiver of her dainty nose, he enquired, "Something amiss?"

"No, indeed. Whatever could be amiss?" The sarcastic sweetness of her voice and her thin smile made him uneasy. "I presume you are waiting up to felicitate me?"

"Felicitate you?"

"On achieving such an estimable alliance! Do you know how many titles he has?" She spat out the list with razor-sharp rapidity. "Duke of Hazlemere, Marquis of Carlsburg, Viscount of Sutton and a baron to boot! Such consequence!" She rolled her eyes, assuming a rather artificially rapturous expression.

"Venetia," he began uncertainly.

"But that would not signify, you must know, if it were not for all those piles and piles of blunt!" She moved by the sofa and gestured extravagantly. "So many estates with all those gardens and riding paths and brooks and stables! Such grand stables with all those magnificent prize horses to choose from. What a dash his wife will cut at all those balls and assemblies and house parties! Just the sort of life you know I long for!'' Her eyes flashed with a burning bitterness. ''I think it is you who must be felicitated, my lord! You have managed to bring the duke up to scratch in a much shorter time than my mama did, you scheming, despicable, odious creature!''

''Venetia, my dear—''

''Don't you 'my dear' me!'' She flung the sofa pillow with such force that it knocked the book from his hand. ''How dare you! How dare you think such things of me!''

Victor had never seen her in such a state and he was becoming alarmed. ''Venetia, I only thought—''

''I know precisely what you thought! Such a pretty opinion you have of me. An empty-headed peagoose with apartments to let!''

''You are out there, Venetia. I never thought such things of you,'' he said soothingly. He watched her anxiously as she paced the room and wondered what he could possibly do to calm her. Perhaps a sip of brandy would help, he thought, quickly moving to pour her a glass.

''You did! You think me all pretension, caring for nothing but inspid balls and the *crème de la crème!* Don't you dare to come near me!'' she shouted as he came towards her with the glass of brandy. ''I hate you!'' She backed away, picking up a dish of bonbons. Victor instinctively stepped backward, but she didn't aim at him. With a resounding crash, the dish shattered against the fireplace and the bon-bons littered the hearth. "You wretch. That you should play me so false." She gave a choking sob and her voice faded.

"Venetia, my sweet, take a sip of the brandy and we can sit down and—"

"Do not use your endearments on me, sir. Save them for your precious Sally!" She took the glass of brandy from him, but it followed the fate of the dish. "Well, she shan't have you! She doesn't love you as I do, and you are my husband, Victor Allen, whether you like it or not! Oh, I hate you!" She looked around and, finding nothing else to throw, snatched a painting from the wall, flinging it at another on the opposite wall where they both fell with a crash to the floor just as the door was flung open by a dumbfounded Charles.

"Victor, I thought I heard..." He stopped, his glance taking in the wreckage. Venetia fled into her room and slammed the door. Charles grinned at Victor. "A lovers' quarrel, my friend?"

Victor, stepping gingerly over the broken glass, felt a little foolish. "She seems a bit out of curl just now. Apparently something about Sally, I apprehend."

Charles's brows rose. "Most unusual behaviour, I should say, coming from a woman known to have silently hid herself away on the occasions when her beloved husband was in the arms of his mistress!"

"Oh, take a damper! And mind your own business!" Victor firmly shoved his friend from the room and shut and locked the door. Venetia's bewildering, rather hysterical behaviour had so rattled him that he could hardly think. But for what Charles had said...

Venetia had certainly not hidden away silently this night! There had been nothing silent about her declaration. *She shan't have you!* If Charles hadn't come in, she might have wrecked the entire room. Victor felt a deep sense of awe and satisfaction as profound relief and overwhelming joy filled him.

Looking down at her recent handiwork, he chuckled. *Perhaps this is where my tempestuous darling belongs, after all. I can't quite feature the Duchess of Hazlemere smashing crockery in a fit of pique!*

He went to her door and tapped gently.

Her voice was muffled, but firm. "Go away."

Victor opened the door and entered to find her lying upon the bed, her face buried in the pillow.

"Such a temper you have, my lady gypsy," he said.

She did not answer.

"Venetia," he said softly, sitting on the bed beside her.

"Go away," she repeated.

"I love you," he whispered in her ear.

"No, you don't. You only say so now because of your conscience. You could have told me I didn't please you instead of going back to Sally—"

He reached for her then and she was too exhausted to resist. He cradled her in his arms, brushed back the hair from her damp forehead and kissed away her tears. "Ah, love. My only love. As if I could even think of any other woman after knowing you."

She sat up. "But you did! You never came to me after...that night! After you had made me realize how much I love you and...oh, Victor, I had never been so happy in my life and I thought...that it was as nothing to you because you had vast experience and—''

His mouth closed upon hers, silencing all speech, all thought. She gave herself over to the exquisite waves of ecstasy that rippled through her limpid body as he kissed her again and again, muttering words of love in his native tongue.

"That night, my darling, was as exciting, as fulfilling and as new for me as it was for you," he told her, "for it was a union of love. The love that I have never had nor will ever have for any other woman save you."

Venetia's heart fluttered with delight at the words she had so feared never to hear. "Oh, my darling Victor!" she cried, her fingers caressing his dear familiar face, only faintly visible in the firelight. She paused as she was struck by recent events. "But if it's true, Victor, how could you have been so willing to divorce me?"

"I was never willing, my sweet. But I was prepared to make any sacrifice for your happiness."

"Happiness? But you did not even consult me!" She abruptly drew away from him. "If you had, you would have learned that I never knew how happy I could be until I met you! You had no right to decide such a thing for me!"

"Hush, my darling," he whispered, drawing her against him once more. "Must we quarrel? I'd much rather do this..." She caught her breath as he peppered kisses against her neck, her throat. "And this..." A throbbing expectancy surged through her as he loosened her nightgown and tenderly caressed her breast. "Shall I show you again how very much I love and want you?" he whispered.

"Oh, yes," she murmured as, swelling with love and a new-found confidence, she unbuttoned his shirt and nestled against his chest. She turned her head to press her lips to his bare flesh and smiled to hear his groan of pleasure.

Hours later Venetia snuggled against Victor, basking in the warmth and magic of his love. She was happier than she had ever been. And this time, Victor could not mistake it for anything but love.

ROMANCE IS A YEARLONG EVENT!

Celebrate the most romantic day of the year with MY VALENTINE! (February)

CRYSTAL CREEK
When you come for a visit Texas-style, you won't want to leave! (March)

Celebrate the joy, excitement and adjustment that comes with being JUST MARRIED! (April)

Go back in time and discover the West as it was meant to be...UNTAMED— Maverick Hearts! (July)

LINGERING SHADOWS
New York Times bestselling author Penny Jordan brings you her latest blockbuster. Don't miss it! (August)

BACK BY POPULAR DEMAND!!!
Calloway Corners, involving stories of four sisters coping with family, business and romance! (September)

FRIENDS, FAMILIES, LOVERS
Join us for these heartwarming love stories that evoke memories of family and friends. (October)

Capture the magic and romance of Christmas past with HARLEQUIN HISTORICAL CHRISTMAS STORIES! (November)

WATCH FOR FURTHER DETAILS IN ALL HARLEQUIN BOOKS!

CALEND

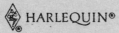

WELCOME TO

The quintessential small town, where everyone knows everybody else!

Each book set in Tyler is a self-contained love story; together, the twelve novels stitch the fabric of the community.

"The small town warmth and friendliness shine through."
Rendezvous

Join your friends in Tyler for the twelfth book, LOVEKNOT by Marisa Carroll, available in February.

Does Alyssa Baron really hold the key to Margaret's death? Will Alyssa and Edward consummate the romance they began more than thirty years ago?

GREAT READING...GREAT SAVINGS...AND A FABULOUS FREE GIFT!

With Tyler you can receive a fabulous gift, ABSOLUTELY FREE, by collecting proofs-of-purchase found in each Tyler book. And use our special Tyler coupons to save on your next TYLER book purchase.

If you missed *Whirlwind* (March), *Bright Hopes* (April), *Wisconsin Wedding* (May), *Monkey Wrench* (June), *Blazing Star* (July), *Sunshine* (August), *Arrowpoint* (September), *Bachelor's Puzzle* (October), *Milky Way* (November), *Crossroads* (December) or *Courthouse Steps* (January) and would like to order them, send your name, address, zip or postal code, along with a check or money order for $3.99 for each book ordered (please do not send cash), plus 75¢ postage and handling ($1.00 in Canada), payable to Harlequin Reader Service, to:

In the U.S.
3010 Walden Avenue
P.O. Box 1325
Buffalo, NY 14269-1325

In Canada
P.O. Box 609
Fort Erie, Ontario
L2A 5X3

Please specify book title(s) with your order.
Canadian residents add applicable federal and provincial taxes.

TYLER-12

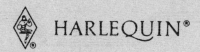

HARLEQUIN®

THE TAGGARTS OF TEXAS!

Harlequin's Ruth Jean Dale brings you
THE TAGGARTS OF TEXAS!

Those Taggart men—strong, sexy and hard to resist...

You've met Jesse James Taggart in FIREWORKS!
Harlequin Romance #3205 (July 1992)

And Trey Smith—he's THE RED-BLOODED YANKEE!
Harlequin Temptation #413 (October 1992)

**Now meet Daniel Boone Taggart in SHOWDOWN!
Harlequin Romance #3242 (January 1993)**

And finally the Taggarts who started it all—in LEGEND!
Harlequin Historical #168 (April 1993)

Read all the Taggart romances!
Meet all the Taggart men!

Available wherever Harlequin Books are sold.

**Harlequin is proud to present our
best authors, their best books and
the best for your reading pleasure!**

Throughout 1993, Harlequin will bring you
exciting books by some of the top names in
contemporary romance!

In February,
look for
Twist of Fate by

Hannah Jessett had been content with her
quiet life. Suddenly she was the center of a
corporate battle with wealthy
entrepreneur Gideon Cage. Now Hannah
must choose between the fame and money
an inheritance has brought or a love that
may not be as it appears.

Don't miss TWIST OF FATE ...
wherever Harlequin books are sold.

BOB1